Puffin Books

An Older Kind of Magic

'Suddenly they all shivered ... they felt something else reaching out from the dark Gardens. Something as old as the thousand-year comet and infinitely lonely ...'

Beneath the earth are older things than perhaps we understand: as old as the ground itself. Every so often, when the thousand-year comet comes around, the ancient spirits appear again above the ground.

Greg knew the comet was coming. Selina, Rupert and Benny knew as well. But they didn't know about the spirits, and their older kind of magic ...

Patricia Wrightson is the recipient of many prestigious awards including the Children's Book Council of Australia Book of the Year Award (four times), the Hans Christian Andersen Medal and an OBE for her services to literature. *An Older Kind of Magic* was highly commended in the 1973 Australian Children's Book of the Year Awards.

ALSO BY PATRICIA WRIGHTSON

The Rocks of Honey
Down to Earth
'I Own the Racecourse!'
The Nargun and the Stars
The Ice is Coming
The Dark Bright Water
Behind the Wind
A Little Fear
Moon Dark
Balyet

FOR YOUNGER READERS

The Sugar-Gum Tree

AN OLDER KIND OF MAGIC

Patricia Wrightson

ILLUSTRATED BY NOELA YOUNG

Puffin Books

Puffin Books
Penguin Books Australia Ltd
487 Maroondah Highway, PO Box 257
Ringwood, Victoria 3134, Australia
Penguin Books Ltd
Harmondsworth, Middlesex, England
Viking Penguin, A Division of Penguin Books USA Inc.
375 Hudson Street, New York, New York 10014, USA
Penguin Books Canada Limited
10 Alcorn Avenue, Toronto, Ontario, Canada M4V 1E4
Penguin Books (N.Z.) Ltd
182-190 Wairau Road, Auckland 10, New Zealand

First published by Hutchinson Junior Books Ltd, 1972
Published by Penguin Books Australia, 1974
10 9 8 7 6
Copyright © Patricia Wrightson, 1972

Made and printed in Australia by
Australian Print Group, Maryborough, Victoria.

National Library of Australia
Cataloguing-in-Publication data:

Wrightson, Patricia, 1921-
An older kind of magic.

ISBN 0 14 030739 7.

I. Title.

A823.3

Chapter 1

There were not many people in the Gardens, for it was a winter afternoon in the middle of the week. Beside the big pond there were only Rupert Potter, Benny Golightly, and Rupert's younger sister Selina. The big cottonwood tree on the lawn above had lost its leaves and become an intricate tower of bare twigs. Behind the kiosk the silk-floss tree was bare too, except for a spray of pink blossom tossed high against the sky. The dark evergreens in beds and thickets threw long, cold-looking shadows. A flock of seagulls swept in from Sydney's harbour and alighted on the grass, mingling with a flock of stout, slow pigeons. Gardeners were spreading loads of fresh soil on empty beds. It was a winter scene.

Rupert had a paper bag of bread-crusts that he had collected at school. He threw a handful into the pond, where the water was moving in soupy swirls like a pot coming to the boil. He and Benny stared hard at the water, and Rupert threw more crusts. A great golden perch leapt up and fell back; the water rocked and boiled.

'There!' shouted Rupert. 'I told you they were whoppers. We ought to bring a couple of lines. Here, Benny, have a go.'

Benny fumbled in the bag, sober as usual. 'There's hardly any left,' he said, extracting a couple of small crusts and looking at them in a slightly worried way.

'You can have mine,' said Selina from behind. She held out her after-school slice of bread and peanut butter. She would not have offered it if she and Rupert had been by themselves, for at those times Selina had no trouble in managing her older brother. It was different when he had Benny, so Selina gave up her bread and peanut butter to please them both.

Benny took it without a thought and tossed it into the water; but by now the perch seemed to have gone away. The bread floated in a mushy way, supported by peanut butter, and two ducks paddled towards it from

6

different sides of the pond. Selina sighed a little as they scooped it up between them.

'I bet that's the first time they've tasted peanut butter,' she said.

'They didn't taste it,' said Rupert, crushing her. 'What about it, Benny? Will we bring a couple of lines in our schoolbags? We could take the fish out in them, too.'

'It's the catching you'd have to watch,' said Benny, heavy with thought. 'That and the eels. They're huge.'

Selina was suddenly cross because her bread had been wasted. No great golden fish had leapt for it, the ducks had not fought over it, and now Rupert said they had not even tasted it. 'You're both mad,' she declared. 'The gardeners are watching people all the time. You know they wouldn't let you.'

But the boys preferred not to know, and went on thinking about plans. A white marble nymph, badly stained by birds, poured a thin, endless trickle of water into the pond. Selina shook the mass of dark hair away from her thin little face and went crossly away.

She knew she would have to go back soon. The sun was making a golden dazzle in the west, the paths were shadowy between the thickets, and all twelve gates of the Gardens were closed at sunset. You could easily get out by pushing aside the rusted iron rods in the top fence, but that meant going home through the Domain, and Rupert might not wait. But the paths and thickets of the Gardens were designed for long walks that didn't go very far. Selina knew she could keep an eye on the boys and run back when they wanted to go.

She passed the fierce statue of 'Retaliation' and turned down towards the kiosk. A thin old man in a shabby

7

coat hurried past holding a limp briefcase under his arm. Selina had often seen him, and she gave him her most winning smile; but he only hurried on and didn't smile or speak. He never did. He just walked through the streets and parks in his shabby coat, with his briefcase so worn that its black had turned to grey, and paused for a second by the garbage bins. His hand would move with the sly, invisible speed of a lizard, his briefcase would flick open and closed, and he would hurry on. Selina could not guess what he collected so passionately and secretly, but she hoped his briefcase was full of it tonight.

The stone wall where the azaleas grow had cut her off from the boys by the pond, and she had to wait till she reached the gateway before she could look again. They were lying down and reaching into the water. She thought they must have met someone else, for there were four boys beside the pond; but then, as she looked again, there were only Benny and Rupert. Selina had just decided to go back after all when she saw the black cat. It was striding over the footbridge across the stream, coming from the direction of the kiosk.

It was a very ordinary cat, thin and dusty-looking like any city stray, with no special marks about it. There was only something firm and decided in its look, something calm and determined in its stride, that made Selina sure it was her cat. It was the one that came to be fed every night, appearing and disappearing within a few minutes. That was all she knew about 'her' cat, and she was astonished and delighted to find it in the Gardens.

The cat gave no sign at all of knowing Selina. There might have been no saucer of milk or scraps every night for weeks. It simply strode by to the end of the wall where the lions sit, and set off across a lawn. Selina was much impressed; yet she couldn't help calling 'Puss!' in the syrupy, coaxing voice people use when an animal ignores them. The cat went on ignoring Selina, but she followed it because she wanted to know where it lived.

It went from one tree or bed to another, but never in a slinking or secret way. It was as different as possible from the old man with the briefcase. Once it strode straight across the middle of a stretch of lawn; and it sat for some time on a large outcrop of sandstone, staring out to sea. Selina almost caught up with it there.

'Puss!' she called again.

The cat moved its tail a little and disappeared.

On its farther side the outcrop of sandstone fell away steeply, with the sea-wall beyond it, and beyond that the crinkled grey water of Farm Cove glinting with winter gold. There were deep clefts across the top of the stone, and on this side a flight of steps set in it, and some little caves hollowed by wind and weather. Selina searched them all. The caves were beautiful with the colours of clean sandstone, cream and gold and brown and red; but they were all empty. There was no sign at all of the cat, and the sun was very low. Selina went running back to the pond. As she went she began to hear, from all round the Gardens, the voice of the city shouting its huge city-song. The great Going Home had begun.

The spinning of tyres, the beating of feet, and the deep, loud droning of the bridge; the grumble and whine of motors; and somewhere, softly, the splashing of fountains. The city roared its song, pouring rivers of cars down every street and rivers of people into every station. Pavements throbbed with the underground rushing of trains. Policemen beckoned, traffic lights flashed, and streets were packed solid. High above Circular Quay little cars ran like strings of beads along the expressway into the pumpkin-gold dazzle of the sun. Trains beat at their rails, buses mooed and howled; the city shouted.

Sir Mortimer Wyvern, caught in a traffic jam in Macquarie Street, looked at the crowds with stern approval. So many people shopping in his great store, buying his evening paper, hurrying home to tune in to his television station; it was a great responsibility, and Sir Mortimer Wyvern knew it. 'They all depend on us, Ash,' he said to his driver's neck. 'They get their living from the city, and the city gets its living from Commerce.'

The neck jerked a little in reply.

The people depended on the city, the city depended on Commerce; but Commerce depended on more people, more and more cars. That was a thought that made Sir Mortimer frown, for there could scarcely be any more cars until there was more room to put them. 'We must have another parking station,' said Sir Mortimer Wyvern.

Another parking station, but where? Every foot of ground in the city was carrying its load of expensive building. If the buildings were not expensive enough, men with bulldozers came at once and tore them down so that more expensive ones could be built. Commerce depended on it. There was barely enough room between the buildings for the cars to run, and no room at all for them to stand. Sir Mortimer's eyes turned to the right, towards the Botanical Gardens: green lawns, and the dignity of trees; paths and pools and quiet statues.

'Fifty acres of sentimental waste,' muttered Sir Mortimer. Even the statue of Governor Phillip was less than twenty feet high. Sir Mortimer frowned at it in a determined way while the traffic lights turned red again, and a shabby old man carrying a limp briefcase crossed the street in front of his shiny car.

'The city can't afford it,' said Sir Mortimer, still frowning. 'I must take it up with the Minister again. We need no more than three acres to begin with.' The traffic lights turned green and the cars moved slowly on.

Rupert and Benny were still standing by the pond, looking for Selina. They were shivering because by now both their shirts were wet. Rupert saw Selina running down between the trees and shouted to her.

'Hurry up, can't you? We're freezing.'

'I saw my cat!' Selina shouted back. She continued to shout as she ran, lowering her voice by degrees as she came closer. 'I think it lives here! I followed it nearly to the top gate, but it got away somewhere. It didn't take any notice of me at all.'

Rupert sneezed. 'Not the same cat, even, I bet,' he said to Benny, and set off for the Macquarie Street gate.

The big, domed central gates were already closed, and a man was just closing the little gates at the side. He pretended to be locking the children in and they went past in a scatter, giggling. Now the city loomed all about them, shutting them away from sunset and sea, and almost from the sky as well. The city made its own landscape of glass-panelled cliffs and towers, all of them lit from inside with pale lights. Between these great masses of concrete and steel and glass, there were still some older buildings of sandstone or brick. A lot of the old ones had stone lions at their steps, bronze eagles over their windows, carved faces or garlands of leaves above their doors. They were old and shabby but somehow grand, quietly waiting for men and bulldozers to come and tear them down. There were hardly any shops in this part of the city; all the buildings were full of offices. The lines of cars, whining and growling, filled your head with noise.

The children reached a corner and waited for a policeman to hold up the traffic. While they waited, they stared at their usual things: Benny at the hairy young men and women who went up the steps of the Library and vanished between its columns; Rupert at a plaque on the wall of the Gardens in memory of horses killed in the war, Selina at a strange fountain that she thought was exactly like a heavy storm inside a jam-jar. They crossed at last, and came very soon to an old building hung with plaster garlands, with a fine shield in the centre. This was where Benny lived with his father; his bedroom window was the one just under the shield.

There were three small shops in the building—at the right a chemist's, at the left a tea-room, and in the centre Golightly's magic shop. Its window was full of tricks and gadgets. There were crawly spiders, sneezing powder, magic pens, and shiny-plastic poached eggs for putting on people's chairs. Rupert and Selina thought it was a splendid shop, but there was no time to look in the window tonight.

'See you,' said Benny, and disappeared into the shop which was not yet closed.

'It *was* my cat,' said Selina at once to Rupert. 'I see it every night. A person knows their own cat, don't they?'

'All right, all right,' said Rupert quickly. 'I don't care if it was. I'm freezing.'

They went on a little way in the criss-cross of narrow streets until, within sight of Benny's building, they came to a wider place where five streets met. Here, taking up the whole of a small city block, was a broad old building of sandstone with tall, deep windows all alight. On three sides it had great doors between granite columns, with lions and unicorns guarding them above. On the fourth side there were two rather secret little wooden doors that nobody ever noticed. The massive walls had little high balconies fenced with curving stone balusters, stout and important. You could not see the roof, for the stone walls rose above it in a way that was a little like the battlements of a castle. In fact the whole building looked more like a shabby old worn-out castle than a home for the Potter family. But Rupert and Selina lived there, with their brother Greg and their mother and father. They were the only people who did; and their large, gentle father was in charge of the whole building.

By day the old Department building was invaded by hundreds of people, and then it seemed to belong to them; but Rupert and Selina were mostly away at those times. At five o'clock the daytime people streamed away; the Department was an empty, shabby castle that belonged to the Potters. There were the cleaners for a little while, but Mr Potter was in charge of them. And there were signs, mysterious and somehow unfriendly, of the people who came by day: a forgotten umbrella, a lost hair-slide, somebody's cough-mixture in a sticky bottle.

Rupert and Selina went in by the side door, under a lion and unicorn and into a white marble lobby. A white marble staircase, fit for ladies in long satin gowns, went soaring up to a far skylight, with broad, high windows lighting every landing. For six floors it went up, turning along each side of the stairwell. To be exact, it was not a white marble staircase above the second floor, but only a concrete one—but the stairwell looked as grand as if it had been marble all the way.

Rupert and Selina did not climb the stairs. In a corner beyond them was an iron cage made of strips of twisted metal, and inside it another iron cage which was an old lift. From this, looking out between the bars, you could watch the floors and corridors slip slowly down as you went very slowly up. Sometimes the lift would pause at one floor and you looked for quite a long time while its door opened and closed, opened and closed, never letting you out. Sometimes you caught only a glimpse of the floor you wanted as the lift went up beyond it, or changed its mind and came slowly down again. At least fifty people grumbled about that lift every day, and for this reason Rupert and Selina preferred it. They knew how to bang on the control panel, or play a tune on the buttons, so that the lift obeyed. It showed that they were different from the day-time people.

Slowly and uncertainly the lift took them up, giving them one view after another of mops and buckets, or of cleaners in overalls. At the sixth floor the children got out. Now there were only skylights above them like large glass tents; yet, when they opened a door near the lift, there was a flight of wooden stairs going even higher. At the top of the stairs there was another door. The children went through it, and came out on the roof of the Department.

Chapter 2

It was a very big roof with a square hole in the centre that
went right down to the ground, where it made a paved
courtyard within the building. If you stood in the street
the Department looked down at you from royal balconies and tall, grand windows in dignified stone walls;

if you stood in the courtyard it closed about you with a crowd of smaller windows in shabby brick walls painted grubby grey and laced with pipes. There was often a heap of waste paper or cardboard cartons waiting to be carted away. From the roof you could not look down into courtyard or street unless you were quite tall, because the edges were walled around to prevent you from falling off.

The courtyard-well cut the roof into sections: a broad square at each end and a long narrow section at each side. One end was filled with skylights and walled off from the rest. The long narrow sections, which the Potters called 'the lanes', made interesting, shut-away places where the children could carry on their own affairs. They led into the broad, open end of the roof that made the Potters' yard, with their house rising above it and a clothes-hoist at one side. There were wooden tubs with some rather sooty shrubs growing in them, and a whole bank of pots with smaller plants. Steps led up to the house, and underneath it, behind the steps, was the laundry.

The whole roof, house and yard, was lifted high above the streets into another level of the city. The arch of the harbour bridge was a distant neighbour; so were the big neon signs mounted on some of the buildings. Taller, newer buildings looked down on it from banks of windows that were empty except in office hours. And here and there, on some of the buildings, lived the people who made up a strange sort of village: those who lived, like the Potters, on windy roof-tops so that they could take care of the buildings underneath. At night their homely little lights winked across the dark canyons of the streets: Mr and Mrs Tipperton, on top of the big Bank building to the south; the Whinberry couple on the old Government building to the west; the Youngs who had a very smart and modern home on the big new Insurance building; and a few others. The Potters were the only roof-top children, but from their windows, through a gap between buildings, they could see Benny's window under the plaster shield.

Rupert and Selina came running along the western lane to its opening, and there Selina suddenly stopped. 'You go in and tell her we're back,' she said. 'If I go I'll have to stop and do something.' Selina played a long game of hide-and-seek in which her mother was always It. Mrs Potter entered into the game with spirit, and the male Potters never interfered. They were able to watch quite calmly because they knew the game was only a game.

'You'll have to come if you're wanted anyway,' said Rupert, and went on across the roof to the lighted kitchen. It was full of a hungry smell of steak-and-kidney, and Mrs Potter was washing up at the sink.

'Go and change that wet shirt before you catch cold,' she said as soon as Rupert came in. 'Where's Selina?'

'In the lane,' said Rupert, who was blue with cold already.

'She can set this table for me as soon as she comes.'

Rupert went in quietly to change his shirt. Just as he had expected, Greg was in their bedroom beginning his evening's homework. He took no notice of Rupert, for he was entranced by a chemical equation that seemed to him to be full of simple beauty. Rupert took off his shirt and pulled on a sweater in respectful silence and went quietly out again: out of the bedroom and out of the house.

Selina had withdrawn farther up the lane. 'She wants you to set the table,' Rupert reported.

'I will, too, when we get back,' said Selina.

They went down the wooden stairs again, and down the main staircase, leaning on the polished banister to slide. They paused to gaze down the stairwell at the floor far below, and up at the skylight above. They stopped on a landing to look face to face at a carved stone head on the old building opposite and, craning downwards through the same window, to get a close-up glimpse of their own lion and unicorn. On the second floor, which was their favourite, they turned off down an empty corridor. This was the time when the Department was theirs, and they were taking possession of it.

There was a hushed, waiting feeling in the old building, as if people were hiding behind all the doors. Sometimes they met a man with a bucket who nodded, or a woman with a duster who smiled; but the cleaners were far apart, and they and the children mostly ignored each other. To the cleaners, Rupert and Selina were the children of the caretaker and best left alone.

At the end of the corridor the children went through a room with a number of desks and out through long double doors on the opposite side. Now they were on one of the balconies. It felt like being perched on the side of a cliff. There were still sunset colours fading and smoky in the sky. Rupert leaned on the stone railing, hooking himself into place with his elbows, and considered how he could steer a course that would bring the Department safely down to the harbour. Selina gazed between curving balusters at the solidness of wall below and the bare twigs of a Lombardy poplar reaching up from the pavement.

'Oh, look!' she cried. 'There's a tiny little lizard—see, near the edge of the stone.'

'I know,' said Rupert very quickly. 'It's Skit—he's mine.' Selina already had the cat, as well as a cockroach called Morris.

'I don't believe you ever saw it before,' she said crossly.

'I tell you, he's mine. He lives at the bottom of that tree, only sometimes he comes up the wall in the cracks. Because it gets warm in the sun, I s'pose. He's a bit late tonight, though—go on home, Skit!'

'Anyhow,' said Selina, 'it's winter, isn't it? He's supposed to be asleep in winter. He shouldn't be awake at all.'

'I can't help that, can I?' demanded Rupert. 'He is awake, you can see that. I s'pose you think I woke him up or something? Go home, Skit.'

The little lizard vanished obediently into the crack. By day he was called Pongo and belonged to six young clerks who fed him with crumbs from their lunch, and sometimes with ants. He didn't mind being Skit at other times, and belonging to Rupert.

The children went back through the lighted office, where Rupert paused beside one of the desks. 'I wouldn't mind a few of those,' he said, looking at a box of very large paper-fasteners. 'They'd be handy for my aeroplane.'

'Have some, then,' said Selina, who really thought the Department belonged to them. 'Here.' She scooped up three or four and held them out.

But Rupert was two years older, and knew better what 'belonging' meant. 'Put them back, Selina,' he said sternly. 'Don't you ever let anyone catch you touching things or there'll be trouble. Go on, put them back.'

'But you took some rubber bands once—and that cardboard thing like a wheel!'

'I didn't know then, about the rubber bands. The cardboard thing was different, they'd thrown it out.'

Selina was sure Rupert was acting like an older brother just to keep her in her place. There were hundreds of paper-fasteners; no one would care about three or four. 'I only wanted them for you,' she said in a sulky voice, and followed him out.

They passed another marble staircase and a more important lift, and came to a long passage with windows looking into the courtyard. Selina stopped to look down in case there were some useful cartons waiting to be carted away and wasted. Rupert hurried on down the passage because he could see old Harry the cleaner, with his polisher.

The polisher was making a strange huffy noise instead of the proper shriek. Harry was switching it on and off, muttering and looking at its lead. Rupert made his face look serious and concerned.

'Hullo, Harry, what's up?' he asked.

From the window Selina heard Harry's angry mumble. He was not exactly talking to Rupert, because he didn't think a man of his age ought to bother explaining adult matters to a child; but he was talking to the polisher with Rupert to listen. Selina went to listen too.

Harry was lean and leathery. He was telling the polisher how useless it was, how many times it had broken down in the last month, how long ago it should have been replaced. As he went on his voice grew louder, his eyes wilder, and his shaggy eyebrows jerked up and down.

The polisher huffled unhappily. It often did this for Harry, though it seemed to work all right for other people.

'Why don't you bust?' roared Harry, kicking the polisher savagely. 'For good and all, why don't you smash up proper? They might get a new one then, they're too mean to do it without.' He kicked it again. 'Can't even do that right, can you? Can't even fall to bits, you whining, miserable . . .' He kicked it again.

At this the polisher's wheezy huffle rose to a shriek, and it shot off in a reeling, drunken course along the passage. Harry rushed after it, choking insults. Rupert and Selina tried to keep their laughter inside themselves as they followed. The polisher swung Harry round a corner and disappeared. A plump, fair woman stopped polishing door-knobs and gazed after them sadly.

'Poor old Harry,' she said. 'He's got his troubles, who hasn't? You wouldn't touch poor Myra's door-knobs, now would you? That's good kiddies.'

Selina smiled as sweetly as she could and waited for Myra to follow Harry round the corner. Then she made a dart for her very favourite room, and Rupert followed a little nervously.

'He'll be in there one of these nights,' warned Rupert. 'He doesn't just come at ordinary times, you know. He's too important.'

'He'd have the door closed,' said Selina confidently. 'He doesn't come much at all.' She went boldly through a smaller room to the larger one beyond. 'I like it in here. It's so tidy.' She stood and looked in a satisfied way at the most private and important room in the whole Department: the Minister's own room.

It had a silky-looking green carpet with an enormous,

bare desk in the middle. There were comfortable chairs of red leather, and bookshelves with neat rows of books, and tall cupboards with polished doors. It was a rich-looking room, and certainly very tidy.

'I'm going out on his balcony,' said Rupert.

From the Minister's balcony you could see one green ridge of the Botanical Gardens; but Rupert could not see it now. In the last few minutes the dusk had turned almost to dark, and Rupert looked out on the city's lights.

Ruthless and strong, the city shut out the rest of the world. Perhaps it shut out even the rain. When rain fell in the city it was distilled, perhaps, somewhere about the twenty-first floor. Now it was shutting out the world with lights—refusing the stars and the moon, and the flat, dark water around it. The steel-and-concrete mountains, the glass-fronted cliffs of daytime, had turned into mountains and cliffs of soft light. To see it, you would never guess it meant merely that the cleaners were in, mopping and polishing five thousand offices. You saw only the magic buildings made of soft light. Around them were hung strings of brighter lights along streets and bridges. Lights floated on the harbour, making patterns of crinkled gold on the black water. Car-lights crawled about like golden insects. Coloured signs flashed like crowns on top of buildings, or were pinned like brooches across the hill of Kings Cross. It was very beautiful. To Skit, the lizard, on his dark wall, it must have seemed like living among the stars; but Sir Mortimer Wyvern knew it was the brilliant light of Commerce. Rupert on the balcony felt more like Skit than Sir Mortimer.

Selina preferred the glory of the Minister's shining desk. She went round to stand by the Minister's chair and looked at his silver inkwell. There was something white on the carpet, in the dark cavern under the desk. Selina picked it up.

It was an old paper-knife, white turning dirty yellow; but it had a very good dragon curled round the handle. Selina guessed some office-girl must have dropped it there. She was sure the Minister would not have an old plastic paper-knife on his desk beside the silver inkwell. 'Finders keepers,' thought Selina, and pushed it up the sleeve of her sweater so that Rupert shouldn't see it. She liked the dragon.

'Hey!' shouted Rupert. 'Come and have a look at this.'

Selina settled the paper-knife in place and went out.

He was standing at one end of the balcony, looking along the side of the Department to an old building that faced it from the front. Selina knew the old building well, of course. It was the grey plaster one with white plaster pillars beside its windows and its front door. There was a sort of porch-roof over the door, with a fierce white eagle on top, spreading its wings. The walls went up past the roof, like those of the Department, and there was a row of white vase-things along the top of the walls.

There was only one window lighted up, and that was the window Rupert was looking at. 'Come and have a look,' he said again. Selina did.

It was like looking at small puppet-stage. She could see just a table with some papers on it, and a stack of bright, oblong shapes, silver and red. There were more of these shapes scattered about the table, some with their silver and red wrappings opened. At the table sat a bearded man with his shoulders bowed and his forehead resting on his hands. He looked very dejected, sitting with the gaily wrapped bars all around him.

'They're sweets or something,' said Selina. 'What a lot! —he must be rich! Is he sick or something?'

'Eaten too many,' said Rupert. 'Serve him right. Fancy buying a stack like that! He could give me some if he can't eat the rest.'

They watched for a while longer, but the bearded man did not move. It was quite dark by now, and at last Rupert said, 'Come on. You've got to set the table.'

They crept quietly out, preferring not to be seen by anyone coming out of that room. Two more passages took them back to their favourite lift, and soon they were on the roof again. Mrs Potter's voice was curling round it like a whip.

'Se-lee-NA!'

Selina slipped quietly into the house, feeling the paper-knife inside her sleeve.

Greg had come out to rest and look at the lights. He was leaning on the wall with his elbows spread, and had looked up thoughtfully when Rupert and Selina arrived. He knew where they had been. A year or so ago, Greg too had gone prowling through the empty Department, and he knew what it felt like: like exploring tribal caves while the natives were out hunting.

Rupert went to climb up on the wall too, for he knew it was all right when Greg was there. Greg watched his struggles for a moment. Then he reached down, grasped the back of Rupert's pants, and heaved with the next jump. Rupert lay on his chest on the wall with Greg still clutching a handful of pants. Flashes of red and green light from neon signs lit up their faces as they leaned there quietly, listening to Mrs Potter scolding Selina in the kitchen. The city hummed to itself below, but there was a sense of quietness here. It was often quiet where Greg was.

After a while the kitchen door opened, spilling yellow light on the roof, and Selina slipped out with a saucepan in her hand. She went down the farther lane to feed her cat and the cockroach Morris. Rupert had theories about them both, so he slid down from the wall to go after her. Greg let him drop with a thud.

Selina was scraping out the saucepan into a tin dish that she kept for the cat. She said, 'It hasn't been yet, has it? Have you seen it?'

'It's not coming,' said Rupert, for this was his theory about the cat—that Selina was just a passing phase with the cat, and one of these nights it would not come. He thought this because its coming was so mysterious, here on the roof above six empty floors. No one knew how it came, so it seemed rather more likely that it would not come at all.

Selina did not bother to argue; she knew the cat would come. She believed in mysterious things, so she finished scraping the saucepan and then took a tiny scrap of milky bread on the spoon for Morris.

There was a shallow drain round the edge of the roof to carry off the rain, and just here it opened into a drain-pipe covered with an iron grating. Morris lived under the grating. Selina balanced his scrap of bread on the edge of it, and waited hopefully. She could never be sure of seeing Morris.

Rupert's theory about Morris was that he was really a large tribe of cockroaches, all living under the grating.

Any one that Selina saw, as long as it was big enough, Rupert believed she would accept as Morris. Selina, of course, believed that she could pick Morris out from a crowd of cockroaches, and that with patience and regular meals he would soon know her too. Now she saw a tiny movement in the dim, reflected light.

'He knows!' she cried delightedly. 'He's come out!' And she planted her foot on the grating to cut off his retreat.

'He's a lighter colour than last time,' said Rupert, peering too.

'He is not a lighter colour. It's just the way he's standing.'

Then the black cat arrived, coming from among the skylights and jumping down from the wall to land beside its dish. Morris flattened himself against the wall and Selina was quiet, listening to the hungry little noises of of the cat's eating; until, from the kitchen, Mrs Potter's voice came exploring the roof.

'Ru-pert! Se-lee-na!'

The cat drew itself together like a spring and leapt back to the top of the wall. Selina picked up the saucepan, and Rupert followed her inside.

The Potters were not a family for talking during meals. Mr Potter, who was large and solid and fair, liked to listen to the news while he ate in an absent-minded way. The news came from the television set in the living-room, but you could hear it in the kitchen if the volume was turned up well. Mrs Potter kept a sharply watchful eye on her family's table-manners; and because of this Rupert and Selina ate in careful silence. Mrs Potter was small and quick, with a heavy mass of dark hair. People always noticed that Selina was very like her mother and Rupert

26

like his father. Greg was like no one: tall and thin, with eyes that were grey instead of blue like his father's. He was often lost in thought, especially during meals; mostly quiet, and yet aware of the people and places around him. He talked most when you were alone with him; then you were surprised at the things he knew and the little things he had noticed.

After dinner Greg went back to his homework. Rupert and Selina washed up, pretending to hate it and making a good deal of noise. In fact, the washing up was one of the reasons why Rupert and Selina were still good friends in spite of Benny. Mr Potter went inside to watch television; and Mrs Potter followed as soon as she was sure that Rupert and Selina had started properly.

'We can't do this tomorrow night,' Selina boasted. 'We're going to Benny's, so we won't be here.'

'You see that you behave yourselves,' said Mrs Potter at once, 'and leave the kitchen tidy, or it'll be the last time. Mind, now. I'll ask Greg when he brings you home.'

So she hadn't forgotten, and that was all right.

Later, when she was going to bed, Selina hid the plastic paper-knife under the paper that lined her drawer. She went to sleep watching the pale flashes of red and green light that washed across her wall from the signs above Circular Quay. Rupert went to sleep watching Greg, who sat absorbed in the circle of light from his desk-lamp.

Greg was the last of the Potters to go to sleep, and first he went out on the roof for a while, to look at the city while he drank a glass of milk.

The air felt like iced water. The buildings were no longer cliffs of light but square, dark mountains. There was just one glowing square on top of the Insurance building—Mrs Young's new bedroom curtains; and one lighted window in the old grey building where the bearded man still sat with his forehead on his hands. An enormous blue toothbrush with white bristles hung in neon lights against the sky. A great cockle-shell turned slowly round and round, red light on one side and white on the other. The arch of the Harbour Bridge was etched in green light. Greg looked up at the sky, searching for the pale stars.

He was thinking of the comet that the papers said was coming next week. It had been here before, they said, a thousand years ago; it would shine in the sky again in another thousand years; and next week it would come. Greg gazed up and thought of that far, pale light journeying on its circle of a thousand years, to pass over the city.

Through dark lanes below, Selina's cat went silently. A thousand years of cat history prickled in its fur. Old mysteries tingled in its whiskers, a witch's spell twitched at its tail; and it padded into the street to sit under the bearded man's window.

Farther off, in an underground tunnel where no trains ran, little brown shadows crept out of the land.

Chapter 3

'Greg,' said Selina, getting up from the breakfast table, 'will you feed my cat tonight? We're going to Benny's.'

'Yes,' said Greg. It was a satisfying answer, simple and complete. No need for Selina to explain where, when or how much; Greg would feed the cat.

'Selina, go and brush that blazer,' Mrs Potter ordered. 'And clean your teeth. Hurry up or you'll be late.'

'Greg,' said Selina from the door, 'will you feed Morris too?'

'No,' said Greg; and that was complete and satisfying too. Selina knew there was no point in coaxing, and Morris would be all right anyway—or Greg would have fed him.

'Go on, Selina. And tell Rupert to hurry up.'

Selina could never be made to hurry until she and Rupert were actually on their way to school. Then she would often cry out that they were late, and make Rupert run to keep her in sight. He had to keep her in sight because it was his job, as her older brother, to see that she arrived safely. It was annoying, and Rupert tried as hard as Mrs Potter to get Selina started in good time.

'Come on, Selina, we'll miss Benny.'

Mrs Potter watched them crossing the roof to the stairs. 'You behave youselves at Benny's.' she called. 'Greg will pick you up at nine o'clock, mind—don't keep him hanging about for you.'

They reached the lift just as it began to go down: one of the daytime people must have arrived early. Rupert at once put his finger on the button, giving it a certain little wiggle. The lift hovered, then rose again obediently. As they came down below the first floor they could see a young clerk staring anxiously up. As soon as the lift stopped he wrenched the door open, determined not to lose it this time. Rupert and Selina stepped out with dignity and walked gravely to the street. As soon as they reached it Selina giggled, said, 'Hurry up or we'll miss Benny,' and began to run.

'Hang on!' shouted Rupert, but she had whisked out of sight round the corner. Rupert pounded after her, and was just in time to see her collide with a tall, bearded, absent-minded young man.

'Selina, you clot!' yelled Rupert, picking up her schoolbag.

Selina was slightly dazed, but the young man hardly seemed to have noticed the collision. He simply removed Selina and went on his way, muttering.

'Crackle-Crunch the super munch,' muttered the bearded man whose name was Ernest Hawke. 'Great heavens!' he shouted. 'I must be going mad!' And he began to cross the street five yards outside the pedestrian crossing. 'Crackle-Crunch will see you through; a something lunch that's good for you. No, no, no!' He stood still in the middle of the street and clutched his beard with both hands.

Cars swerved, tyres squealed, and a frightened driver yelled, 'Don't you want to live, mate?'

'Follow your hunch; try Crackle-Crunch,' muttered Ernest Hawke, and groaned deeply. He finished crossing the street, and stood on the steps of the old grey building to think. Then he wandered up to his office on the first floor and stood by the window, looking out at the roof where the white eagle spread its wings.

Everything in his office was as he had left it the night before: his precious cameras, the sheets of paper scribbled with slogans, the bars of Crackle Crunch wrapped in silver and red. On the wall, to inspire him, was a picture of a huge, ideal Crackle-Crunch. Ernest Hawke sat down and stared at it. He stared at the giant slabs of pink biscuit and the stiff white cream between, with bits of chopped nuts sticking out of it; he made himself stare with longing at the dark glaze of chocolate on the outside. He made himself say 'Crackle-Crunch' hungrily. Then he put his forehead on his hands and groaned.

It was making him feel sick again.

'That man,' Selina was saying as she and Rupert reached their school. 'The one with the beard.'

'The one you nearly knocked down,' said Rupert.

'He's the one we saw in the window last night, with all the sweets or whatever they were.'

'Even if he was, it's still no reason for knocking him down.'

Benny's father was going out to dinner that night. Rupert and Selina were going home with Benny after school to keep him company for some of the time. They were both excited about it; but of course they knew they would have to wait in the Botanical Gardens until the magic shop was closed. They expected the time to drag, but in fact it went quite quickly.

They came in from the Domain through Victoria Lodge Gate, and went straight down to the sea-wall to watch for little jellyfish at the shallow edge of Farm Cove. Selina showed them the rock where her cat had disappeared, and Rupert pointed out that it had probably just gone to the lodge. They went on to the pond, and as they reached it they began to hear the voice of a crowd.

'Demonstration!' cried Rupert. 'Come on!'

There were often demonstrations to be seen from the Gardens, and the children always found them fun to watch. The people marching with banners that they would never let you read, looking excited and important as they marched. The policemen who came with them to make sure there was no trouble, and made it look even more exciting. The rather wild man who talked for a long time into a microphone, always saying the same sort of thing. The people who listened for a little while and went away; the people who never seemed to notice at all. The television van, getting it all on film for the news and making it look so real, Selina said.

'I hope they still have demonstrations when I grow up,' she added wistfully.

'Can *you* see what it's about, Benny?' Rupert asked.

'They keep turning them round . . . Ted Someone, I think.'

'Whatever it is,' said Selina, 'they'll fix it.'

'Well,' said Rupert, 'no one's going to start a row this time. I'm going back to the pond.'

They went by the main path. A few people were sitting on benches in the late sun; one or two small children waddled over lawns. The African yellow-wood was lit all over with small yellow fruit, like lighted windows on a dark green mountain. Drifting from behind it came the shabby old man with his shabbier briefcase. Benny stopped.

'That old bloke,' he said soberly, 'he could be famous. He's *good*. He'd make the best stage-magician in the business.'

'Go on,' said Rupert.

'No, honest. Look, I'll show you.'

They knew Benny had a serious interest in stage magic and studied it soberly. They followed him over the lawn after the old man, who was drifting like a leaf towards the kiosk.

'You want to watch his hand,' said Benny, 'when he

33

stops near a garbage-bin. You're looking straight at it, but you'll hardly see it move. Watch, now.'

The old man glanced over his shoulder and drifted a little faster.

'Sometimes,' said Benny, leading them on, 'he'll even get his briefcase open without you seeing. And he's not even using any patter or business to take your eye off. He's just brilliant, that's all.'

The old man, looking hunted, whisked out of sight round a bank of hydrangeas.

'Round here,' said Benny, absorbed and still leading. 'I wish he'd teach me. I'd be rich.' They followed him round the hydrangeas, where they all stopped dead.

The old man stood at bay with his lips drawn back in a snarl. His eyes glared, and even his hair seemed to bristle. He looked like a very dangerous rat. The children were frozen, Benny turned his own shade of rusty red under his freckles—and while they stood confused, the old man performed one more conjuring trick. He vanished.

'Gosh!' gasped Rupert. 'Wasn't he wild?'

Benny was distressed. 'I didn't mean to upset him—I just thought he was so good—Oh well, that's that, I s'pose. He doesn't like being watched.'

'He must be doing something wrong, then,' said Selina with spirit. She was defending Benny; but Benny couldn't allow it.

'You can't do much with rubbish-bins. What he's doing, he doesn't want it to be seen, that's all. He's got a right.'

Rupert took him down to the pond to recover. Selina went back to the big rock to have one more look for her cat; she had not wanted to look while Rupert and Benny were there, in case Rupert made fun of her to Benny. She looked in all the cracks and holes within reach and found no sign of the cat. It seemed to have disappeared as cleverly as Benny's old man. Selina sat for a while on the steps that were let into the stone, gazing at the soft colours inside one of the little caves; letting the rich, gay afternoon soak into her mind. The little jellyfish that you could almost see through; the demonstration with its banners; the golden fruit on the yellow-wood tree; the old man, frightening them off like a jew-lizard; the magic shop, still to come. A grey shadow moved over the rock and made her jump. She giggled a bit and got up from the cold steps, for the shadow had startled her. She had thought it was a little grey hairy man, with claws instead of fingers and toes.

As Selina ran back to the pond, the city began to bellow its evening song again. It sounded impatient, as if it wanted to get rid of all the people so that it could get on with spinning its web of lights for the night. Already it had spread over itself a light, hazy mist of fumes and vapour, very beautiful. 'Go home, go home!' it bellowed. 'There's magic to be done!'

Selina could see the boys by the pond with two other boys; but when she arrived there were only Rupert and Benny. Rupert was watching her come, impatiently.

'Who were the others? she said. 'Where did they go?'

'What are you talking about?' said Rupert. 'I wish you wouldn't go off at the last minute. We always have to wait.'

Selina followed them to the gate feeling irritated and a bit foolish. She was seeing too many people lately.

The magic shop was still open when they reached it. The woman who ran the tea-shop was just bolting its doors. 'Company tonight, eh?' she said as they passed. 'I'll be keeping an ear to you, mind.' And she smiled widely, to show that it would be a friendly ear. In the magic shop Mr Golightly was doing something at the till, his lips muttering silently and his sandy hair standing up. He always had the same slightly worried look that Benny often had; it always made Selina a little anxious for him, and eager to please. She and Rupert stood politely behind Benny, waiting for Mr Golightly to finish.

In front of him, the glass showcase was filled with the same sort of tricks as the window. Behind him, a bunch of hideous masks hung down from the shelves. A small table was piled with clawed and hairy hands, meant to be worn like gloves. A plastic toad squatted on one shelf beside a plastic skull. With the daylight shut outside and the light switched on, it looked wonderful. Rupert and Selina thought it was the most magic place in the city.

Mr Golightly closed the till, looked up and discovered the children.

'Selina,' he said politely. 'Rupert,' he added. To Benny he said, 'Take them upstairs. Dinner's in the oven. Pies.' He looked worried. 'I hope you like pies, Selina? Rupert? Benny does.'

Selina said, 'Oh, *yes*, Mr Golightly,' very eagerly. Rupert said, 'Pies—super!' Benny said, 'We'll have it when you're gone.'

'I hope it won't get too dry,' said Mr Golightly with misgiving. 'You'll be all right tonight, will you? Not nervous? I won't be late, you know, and Mrs Chafer will be keeping an ear.'

36

'Oh, no, Mr Golightly, we love it here,' said Selina. 'And Greg's coming at nine. It won't be long enough.'

'Can we look at the shop while you're getting ready?' asked Rupert as usual.

'You show them, Benny,' said Mr Golightly, and went out through the storeroom behind the shop. Soon they heard the swishing noise of a shower overhead.

Rupert and Selina were already exploring the showcase. Benny closed the door of the shop and came to watch.

'What's this?' cried Selina, picking up a strip of fur with glistening eyes at one end.

'It crawls up your arm,' said Benny, and showed her how.

'What do you do with these?' asked Rupert, examining two little balls in a box.

'One bounces and the other doesn't,' said Benny. He bounced one, palmed it neatly, and passed the second to Rupert. He was very neat and expert with all the tricks, and showed one after the other as Selina or Rupert chose.

'You're awfully good,' Selina said. 'Isn't he, Rupert?'

Benny went rusty pink with pleasure and said, 'I'll show you my magic-bag after dinner.'

Mr Golightly came down in an overcoat and scarf. 'Finished here, have you?' he said anxiously. 'That's right, the pies will be burning ... That goes on the bottom shelf, Benny, are the legs spread out properly? ... Now you won't make a noise and upset Mrs Chafer, will you? Selina, you won't let the boys be too rowdy?'

'Oh, no, Mr Golightly, we won't make a sound.'

'Of course you won't, I know I can trust you. Up you go then, and I'll put the light out as I leave.'

There were piles of boxes in the storeroom. A door

led out to a courtyard at the back, which was the way into Benny's place when the shop was closed. A flight of stairs led to the rooms above, and the children clattered up them into the warmth of Benny's kitchen. Behind them the light in the shop went out; the grinning masks, the hairy hands, the spiders, toads and skulls, all disappeared into the darkness and waited. They heard the storeroom door close. All the flat, and the shop underneath, was theirs at last.

'Wow!' yelled Rupert. 'I smell pies!'

'There's tomato sauce somewhere,' said Benny, and disappeared into a cupboard.

Selina threw up the kitchen window and leaned out. 'Hello, Mrs Chafer!' she called.

'Shut that window, Selina, it's cold,' said Rupert. 'You're supposed to be keeping us quiet. "Oh, *yes*, Mr Golightly, we won't make a *sound*, Mr Golightly." Erk!'

Selina flushed. 'Well, I like Mr Golightly. And I can't keep Benny quiet when it's his house and I'm just a visitor. Can I, Benny?'

'Eh?' said Benny, emerging from the cupboard. 'There's a whole bottle, I knew there was.' He put a large bottle of tomato sauce on the table.

The pies were very brown from being in the oven so long. The children covered them in a red blanket of tomato sauce. Benny made cocoa and found some apples. Selina washed up and the boys dried. Perhaps they made enough noise to reach Mrs Chafer's ear, but at least it stopped them from hearing if she protested. Afterwards Benny showed them his magic-bag.

First he turned it inside out to show that it was empty. Then he took out of it an Australian flag, a plastic egg,

and a rubbery snake. When he had made them all vanish
again and the bag was empty, he showed the cunning
pockets in which the things were hidden. Rupert examined the bag with Selina leaning over him and saying,
'Let me—Let me . . .' Benny watched them and remembered an old dream that he had never told to anyone:
that some day there would be a magic-bag without
pockets, a trick that was real instead of only clever.

Because they were still absorbed in the bag, they
happened to hear a knocking at the storeroom door.
'Greg!' cried Selina. 'It's not nine o'clock yet!'

'Of course it is, you nut, look at the clock,' said Rupert,
just as surprised. Benny had already gone to open the
door.

In a minute Greg came in with two coats over his
arm. He handed them to Rupert and Selina. 'You'll want
these. It's cold out.' While they put the coats on he said
to Benny, 'Mum says can you come to dinner tomorrow
night?'

'Wow!' yelled Rupert. 'Can you, Benny?'

Benny had turned pink again. 'Is it all right if I ask?' he
said. 'Dad's not here.'

'We'll expect you when we see you,' said Greg. 'Don't
come down, I'll shut the door.'

As they went downstairs Selina said, 'Can we go home
the long way, Greg? Round the streets?'

Since she always did ask this, Greg and Mrs Potter had
allowed for it. Her own quiet part of the city—the great,
silent office-blocks and the tangle of small, dimly lit
streets—had no night-magic for Selina; but just two
blocks away were the streets where magic never stopped.
There were the signs that promised you anything from a

wooden leg to an ocean cruise—the theatres—the people rushing by in cars or strolling on foot, not to work but to be free and have fun. There, above all, were the shop windows—magic caves full of light and colour, where make-believe people showed you how wonderful life could be if you could pay for it. Selina loved those make-believe people with their long, stiff eyelashes and glistening hair. She loved them best when they were doing things: bending back at unlikely angles, or taking woolly dogs for walks; showing off their swimming gear to each other, or holding their hats in a make-believe wind. But whether they were doing things or just standing in wonderful make-believe rooms she loved their petrified smartness, and their happy, petrified smiles, and the beautiful things they wore or used. They were storybook people, and the fairy godmother was somewhere in the shop.

Even Rupert liked going home the long way, because he liked being out late among the people. And it took ten or fifteen minutes instead of three.

'Did the cat come?' Selina asked as they went. 'Did it eat everything?'

'Most of it,' said Greg. 'Went off with a bit in its mouth for later.'

Selina stopped dead. 'Did it? It's never done that before!'

'Someone else must've fed it first,' said Greg.

Selina did not argue because they had reached Australia Square, and she was watching the fountain changing colour. 'Can we go past Wyverns'?' she asked. 'They have lovely windows.'

'You know we go past Wyverns',' said Rupert. 'But I'm not standing round while you stare in every window.'

They went slowly past Wyverns', and Selina did not stop until they came to a window that was furnished as a kitchen. There were tables loaded with brilliant china and shining pans; and one of the petrified people stood with a hand resting lightly and daintily on a stove. What caught Selina's eye was the bright-coloured fruit that decorated the wall; that would be a lovely thing to have in your kitchen, she thought.

The window was the one beside the doors of the shop. They were closed, of course, but Selina went into the doorway to see the fruit from that side. Rupert and Greg waited a little, not very patiently. They were all startled when a small side-door opened and two men were suddenly close to them, talking.

'Yes, Sir Mortimer,' said the first very respectfully. 'On Tuesday evening, Sir Mortimer.'

'I'll look in before the meeting,' said the second, coming out in the street. He had a smooth, narrow face and wore a coat as beautiful as any in the windows. He got into the back seat of a car that was parked at the kerb and was driven away. The small door was closed and locked.

'Sir Someone,' whispered Selina, impressed. 'He had a man to drive him—did you see, Greg?'

'Sir Mortimer,' Rupert put in. It was a name he had heard mentioned once or twice. 'Isn't he the one that owns the shop? Sir Mortimer Wyvern?'

'That's him,' said Greg. 'Must be working late, and now it's his bedtime. Yours, too.' He led them off.

They went back down another street, one that would lead them to the front of the Department. It seemed very dim after the brightness of Pitt and George Streets. 'Cross here,' said Greg, watching for car-lights.

As they crossed the street, Rupert suddenly said, 'What's that?'

'Where?' said Greg, keeping steadily on.

'Something came up out of the gutter—it's gone now.'

'Selina's cat, probably.'

'It was bigger than that,' said Rupert uncertainly. They reached the gutter, and he bent down to look. 'There's just a grating...'

'A rat, then,' said Greg, grinning. 'Some rat—bigger than a cat, was it?'

Rupert said nothing. He had thought that whatever came out of the grating was as big as a person of six, but older. Much older. Yet there was no one in the street at all.

They went in through one of the little wooden doors at the side of the Department. There was no light showing in the old grey building, beside the outspread wing of the white eagle. Ernest Hawke had gone rushing away hours ago, muttering 'Crackle-Crunch' in tones of hatred. They did not see Selina's cat sitting under the wing of the eagle and staring at his window.

Chapter 4

'Bags I work the lift!' cried Rupert, rushing ahead.

Selina was shocked. 'You have to let Benny if he wants to. He's the visitor.'

'I know that, twit. I said, bags I show *Benny* how to work it.'

'He can already. Can't you, Benny?'

Benny had been shown the tricks of the lift, but he felt his position as a guest and did not like to say so. They were earlier than usual in coming from the Gardens. They had come at the first possible moment, as soon as the city began roaring and grumbling, so that Benny could share in exploring the haunted, empty Department. Rupert was also eager to show Benny his plane. He kept rushing ahead a little way, then stopping while Benny caught up. He was waiting now, by the bare Lombardy poplar at the front door of the Department. People were still coming out, hurrying down the pavement, waiting for the street-lights, or launching themselves dangerously into the traffic. Rupert stood out of their way against the tree.

Suddenly he stiffened, and his face went red. 'What's up?' said Selina, coming up with Benny.

Rupert said nothing, but pointed with the toe of his shoe. Benny and Selina looked.

On the dull black pavement lay a small black shape, neatly curved. It was the body of a very small lizard, squashed quite flat.

'Who is it?' said Benny. He was not a pet collector himself, but he knew enough not to say 'What is it?'

'Skit,' said Rupert heavily. 'I thought he was staying up on the wall for the winter.'

'He might have fallen off,' Selina suggested in a small voice. She had never had a pet squashed, and was not sure what to say.

'Fallen off!' Rupert's voice was bitter. 'He's a lizard, not a stupid cockroach . . . He was going home when some clumsy great coot trod on him . . .'

'Are you going to put him on the tree?' Selina asked

in an even smaller voice. 'You can't leave him there . . .'

Rupert felt in his pocket and took out a matchbox. He slid out the tray and scraped the little body into it. It slid in like a plastic lizard from Golightly's magic shop: stiff, flat and neatly curved.

'We could bury him,' said Benny. 'We could easy scrape a hole at the bottom of the tree, just under the edge of the asphalt. There's no one about.'

All the people had indeed drained suddenly away, as going-home crowds do. The street was as quiet as it ever would be. But Rupert needed a better place than a hole in the pavement; he needed a grand tomb for Skit, to make up for his being squashed. He just went on frowning at the street.

Selina knew what he needed. 'The eagle,' she said, pointing to the great white eagle above the porch of the old grey building across the street. Rupert looked at it uncertainly, still frowning.

Selina took the matchbox from his hand, marched to the corner and waited for the traffic lights to change. Then she crossed, and the boys followed, Rupert hissing 'Selina!' as he went.

On the other side, Selina strolled up the pavement watching for people as she went, till she reached the grey building. Its front door was closed, but there were windows to the left that were still open at the top. Selina wandered up the steps between two pairs of white columns. Above her was the porch-roof that the columns supported; and above that, of course, was the eagle. Selina leaned against one of the rear columns, while the boys looked nervously at her and the street in turns.

The rear columns were very near the wall of the building. Though they were smooth and round, each ended in a square base about two feet high. Selina placed her foot on a corner of this base—and suddenly swung the other foot across to a broad window-sill. With the matchbox in her blazer pocket, and clinging to the column, she managed to climb to the top of the lowered sash. Crouching there, she spared time to look down and wrinkle her nose triumphantly; for she was a better climber than Rupert, but he always refused to admit it.

He could not have admitted it just then. Between admiration, horror at Selina's cheek, and dread that she might fall or break the window, he could hardly breathe. He watched her stand up carefully, one hand on the column and the other reaching up to grip the edge of the roof. She groped about, feeling for the eagle's wing, and took the matchbox from her pocket.

At his window above, Ernest Hawke was transfixed. He had been standing by his table, staring gloomily down at the porch-roof, when a very small hand came groping over the edge of it. Another small hand came patting about at the wing of the eagle; then, after one or two tries, a matchbox was tossed behind the great plaster wing. Ernest Hawke reached his window in time to see a dark head swing across to the steps below, and two figures on the pavement suddenly go limp. Rupert was saying 'Selina!' again.

Ernest Hawke clutched his beard. For the first time in several days he clutched it hopefully. He had had a shock, and now he could feel his brain coming to life again. 'They'll go anywhere for Crackle-Crunch,' he murmured, trying it out.

Rupert, Benny and Selina raced back across the street

46

on a gale of giggles. Skit's sad little death had turned into a victory because of the grandeur of his funeral. Since it was still early, they went running to the secret wooden door of the Department and disappeared inside. Ernest Hawke watched them go.

Inside the Department, they made their way by back stairs and roundabout passages in case any daytime people were still about. Selina's unlikely success had put them in the mood for giggling: even Benny's rare 'Hoo-hoo-hoo' joined in. They came out on the roof in a noisy bunch, just as Mrs Potter expected. She was ready for them.

'Se-lee-na! Ru-pert! Bring Benny in for some cocoa . . . We can't have dinner till Mr Potter sees to the cleaners and locks up, Benny, so have this to keep you going . . . Selina, I want you to give me a hand with the table before you go off. Rupert, what are you doing with Benny?'

Rupert knew better than to disappear with Benny while Selina was setting the table. 'We're going to look at my plane,' he said. Selina stopped giving him dark and threatening looks, and relaxed.

'And then?'

'Then . . . we're going down to the courtyard, to see if there are some more boxes I can use.'

'Mind you don't cart up too much useless rubbish, then. Selina, go and change that tunic.'

The plane was stored in the mouth of the lane where Selina fed her cat. Benny was gravely interested in it, especially in the hinged wing-tips that Rupert was inventing and building into it. They were meant for evasive action, and Rupert explained the theory.

'You don't want to get away from somebody underneath you; you've got the drop on him already. It's the one that comes down at you out of the sun, he's the trouble, see? So you just drop your wing-tips, see, and then you drop down out of range and scoot off. They don't just drop, of course, the air'd keep them up. You have to wind them down.'

'Would those hinges hold?'

'Well—you'd have to get the right sort, of course——this is just the first model, you know. When it comes to testing, the right sort of hinges ought to be easy. What's harder, I don't really know how much of the wing ought to be hinged. You know—how much drop you'd get to the foot.'

'You need a book. Aeronautics or something.'

'There's nothing in the library at school. And I've only got twenty-five cents.'

'You can get books pretty cheap from some of the second-hand places. I know a few. We could look on Saturday.'

They examined the frame, the joints, the box seat. Rupert held forth about wind-lift and currents. They talked about testing the model by gliding from the roof across to the Botanical Gardens.

'You'd be breaking some law, I s'pose,' said Benny gloomily.

Selina came, running with a speed that suggested an escape from her mother. They took Benny downstairs, pausing to show him the stone face on the building over the street.

'Isn't it like Mrs Chafer?' said Selina.

They found a plastic butterfly off somebody's hair-slide, and gave it to Benny for his magic-bag. They tracked old Harry through the corridors again, until they found

48

him in trouble with the polisher; then they stood by innocently until Harry was dragged off round a corner shrieking, 'I'll learn you yet, you . . .' After that they set off to show Benny the window where the bearded man had sat so miserably over his sweets.

'And the very next day I ran into him,' said Selina. 'Don't make a noise, we have to go through the Minister's room.'

The outer door was closed. Selina opened it very gently while Rupert hissed 'Selina—don't', and they crept in, shocked at their own daring. The second door was open, though. They went towards it quietly, intent on impressing Benny, and were frozen with astonishment to hear voices from the Minister's room. They just stood there, partway across the outer room.

The first voice sounded tired, or perhaps worried. 'What you say may be very true, Sir Mortimer,' it said. 'The free movement of traffic, with the increasing number of vehicles, is certainly one of the city's worst problems. What I question is your solution to the problem. I don't think it's a solution at all, in fact, but something much more dangerous. An easy way out.'

'Dangerous?' said the second voice. It was not tired or worried, but sure of itself. You could tell it was prepared to argue for a while and then win.

'The Botanical Gardens,' said the first voice, 'are important to the city, and to people beyond the city. They are surely one of the services that a city supplies to the people—that a city *exists* to supply. If we absorb this land, bit by bit, we are surely removing one of the reasons for the city to exist at all. We are in danger of killing the city in order to keep it alive.'

49

'Oh, come, Mr Minister,' said the second voice, 'you and I are practical men. It is Commerce that keeps the city alive, not some ideal of service to the people. The city's business is making money, and this is the service the people expect from it. They will very soon tell you that. Which would upset the people more, do you think? Losing money, or losing part of the Gardens?'

'You may have some trouble,' said the Minister dryly, 'in proving that the people have lost any money at all; whereas the loss of the Gardens . . .'

'Of a part of the Gardens, sir.'

'—of a part of the Gardens to begin with, will be a hard fact in front of their eyes.'

'There again, Mr Minister, you and I are practical men. We know that what the people think will depend on what they are told. On good Public Relations, sir. We can prove to the people that they are losing money, so long as no one begins unfairly by telling them that they are losing the Gardens. That is why I have asked you for confidential talks.'

Benny, Rupert and Selina were so surprised to hear their Minister talking about their Gardens that they had forgotten to creep away. They had even crept a little closer to the door. The name of Sir Mortimer sounded familiar; but now the Minister was talking again.

'Fortunately, Sir Mortimer, the problem is not really mine. You will need to discuss it with the City Council, and with other members of the Government. My own problem is to protect the Gardens: for my Government and for the people. I will do my best to protect them, Sir Mortimer.'

'I think,' said Sir Mortimer, 'that you will find my

proposal is accepted. I am not speaking for myself alone. I represent Commerce, Minister. I thought it fair to discuss the matter with you now, and I hope you will be as fair. Serious damage could be done if the people heard ... Great heavens! What is that?'

Benny had breathed too heavily. A dark, smooth face appeared at one door, and a flurry of children disappeared at the other. Sir Mortimer Wyvern turned on the Minister.

'Children,' he said accusingly. 'Eavesdropping.'

'Children?' said the Minister, astounded. Since he never saw or heard of them, he had quite forgotten there were children anywhere in the Department.

'Five or six of them,' declared Sir Mortimer. 'At least two of them were very dark, with white beards.' As soon as he had said it, he knew there was something unreliable about this. He coughed in an embarrassed way, and passed his hand over his eyes. What *had* he seen? he wondered. For a moment he had been sure there were five or six fleeing children, and at the rear two or three who were very dark and had flowing white beards.

'My dear Sir Mortimer ...'

'Excuse me, Minister,' said Sir Mortimer unhappily. 'This quaint old building of yours is inclined to be dark. The shadows, perhaps ...'

'Of course,' said the Minister kindly. 'I often see astonishing things here myself; and only the other day an ivory paper-knife that I value ... In any case, if there were any children, I hardly think they could understand what we were saying.'

Rupert, Selina and Benny were not trying to understand yet. They were down in the courtyard, where they should have been all along; and frozen with horror as they imagined the Minister going in search of Mr Potter. They were not sure how they had reached the courtyard, but having got there they could do nothing more just now. 'Do you think he saw us?' whispered Selina at last.

'Sure to,' said Benny.

'Well . . .' said Rupert. 'We were pretty quick, you know. I never went so quick in my life. He might've seen just a sort of flash, and not who it was. Anyhow, we'll soon know.'

When they had thawed a little more they took two boxes from the courtyard as an alibi and went back to the roof. They were very quiet. Selina would have forgotten to feed her pets if Mrs Potter had not shown her a saucepan of scraps she had collected. They all went quietly off with the saucepan, down to the end of the lane.

They found they were breathing again. Rupert consulted Benny about the cockroach Morris, whether it really was a single cockroach or a whole swarm that had fooled Selina. Benny considered and said, 'Well, it's her cockroach anyhow,' which left the question open. The black cat came, leaping down from the wall and springing back among the skylights. Benny was deeply absorbed in the whole mystery of the cat. Yet all the time they felt the weight hanging over them.

Once Selina said, 'It was that Sir Mortimer Wyvern. We heard him talk last night, with that springy voice.'

'Shush!' said Rupert; and they wriggled uneasily.

When Mrs Potter called them to dinner ('Ru-pert! Se-lee-na!') they went so quietly that she looked at them in a worried way. They didn't notice, for their eyes kept swivelling to Mr Potter, large and silent in his overalls, listening to the news.

The news finished at last, and Mr Potter's blue eyes passed with brief satisfaction over his family until they came to Benny. Then he said 'Benny' in greeting. Benny went rusty pink and smiled timidly. Mr Potter said nothing more; all the children relaxed at last.

Then Greg had one of his rare talkative moments and told them about the comet that was coming. Mr Potter had heard about it on the news, but he didn't say so; he just listened with enjoyment. Mrs Potter said, 'You'll be wanting to watch for that, Greg. And how many thousand years do those things last?' To Rupert, Selina and Benny the comet sounded exciting and unreal. They still felt the pins-and-needles of relief, and would have liked to giggle.

They did giggle a good deal later, while Benny was helping with the washing up. Mrs Potter was relieved at the noise, and called out sharply from the living-room. 'Now then, you two,' politely ignoring Benny because he was a guest, 'not too much noise. Greg's trying to work.'

They went on giggling and washing up until, all at once, Selina was quiet. 'They want to take some of the Gardens,' she said, very softly. 'For a road or something. It's a secret.'

'We know that,' said Rupert, waiting. He knew it had to be worked out.

'The Minister's in charge of the Gardens. That's funny.'
Benny nodded.

'He won't let them,' said Selina.

'He might have to,' said Rupert.

'Oh no,' said Selina with confidence. 'The Minister's on our side, he's nice. He won't let them.'

Chapter 5

On Saturday morning Benny and Rupert were going to buy a book on aeronautics.

'I'm coming too!' cried Selina hopefully.

'Oh, Selina,' said Rupert, 'can't Benny and I go *anywhere* on our own? You don't know anything about planes.'

The fact was that Rupert was in two minds about this book-buying idea. It did seem a proper and serious way to go about designing a plane; on the other hand, he was afraid it mightn't work, and he would rather Selina wasn't there when it failed.

'Selina's going to Woolworth's for me,' said Mrs Potter at once. 'I've got a list.'

'It's not fair!' cried Selina. 'Why do girls have to do everything?'

'You like going to the shops,' said Mrs Potter firmly.

It was no use denying that, but Selina still felt hurt and left out; so she flounced off with her string bag, deciding to take a long time and have a good look at the shop windows.

Rupert and Benny set off towards Circular Quay, for Benny knew of two or three second-hand bookshops in that area. He led the way through narrow lanes and little 'places' that the Saturday-morning crowds never reached.

'I've got fifty cents now,' said Rupert. 'Will they really have a book for that, do you think?'

'I've got fifty cents I can lend you,' said Benny.

'Trust you,' said Rupert gratefully. He grew more hopeful at once, and invented a way of hopping along with one foot on the narrow pavement and one in the gutter.

The pavement was narrow because this was one of the little 'places'. As Benny walked, his right shoulder brushed against a wall of strong wooden hoardings; and out of it rose one of the older buildings of the city, imprisoned in a cage of steel framing. It was being converted into something newer and bigger. Somewhere high up in the building, a monster machine sang two giant notes, over and over, as it worked. On the ground underneath, an electric drill chattered, harsh and hysterical. At a gap in the hoardings the boys stopped to watch. They could not talk because of the shrill, hard clatter of the drill. They just watched.

It was a shadowy place, under the old building and inside the hoardings. On the farther side of it, the drill was leaping and shrieking and shaking. The boys watched narrowly. It had already been at work on the ground near at hand; Benny pointed to a hole filled with broken concrete and stone. Above them, the giant machine changed from its high note to its low one. Since they could not talk, Rupert wanted to act. He made himself tall, and strode behind the hoardings. He clumped across the broken rock while Benny waved his arms to call him back.

Suddenly Rupert stumbled. He turned a startled face to Benny and seemed to drag himself up. Then he came quickly back outside the hoardings.

'Something grabbed my foot,' he gasped. 'Something *pulled*.'

Benny said nothing. There was nothing to say. They went on, not looking at each other, until they came to the shop in the street beyond.

It was a very large bookshop and packed, upstairs and down, with old books. Most of them looked and smelt so shabby that Rupert's hopes rose again. He explained what he wanted to a young man who said, '*Aerodynamics*,' and showed him where to look. Rupert took a book from the shelf and began to look at it, while Benny wandered away into the basement.

Rupert decided to begin by looking at prices. They

were a shock. As far as he could see, the cheapest book on aerodynamics was three dollars; he could not guess what it must have cost when it was new. He thought he might cunningly find out about wing-tips without actually buying the book, so he turned over the pages. They were full of diagrams with letters and symbols, and there seemed to be nothing to show what they meant. There were words that were probably meant to explain, but they did not explain anything to Rupert. He was struggling with his third book when he heard heavy breathing at his shoulder, and found that Benny had come back.

Benny was looking worried and dogged, and clutching a flat parcel. 'I can't lend you the money,' he confessed. 'Not now.'

'Oh well,' said Rupert, 'it's no use, then.' He put the aerodynamics book back on the shelf. He was really very relieved.

'I'll go home and get some if you like,' said Benny, still dogged. 'Only I had to use this lot. I needed it.'

'It wouldn't have been enough anyway,' said Rupert. 'You can't get anything decent for a dollar.' He looked coldly at Benny's parcel.

Benny turned his own shade of rusty pink. 'If it's any good I'll show you later.'

'Well, I don't want to know, for heaven's sake. Come on, then.'

'You could go to the Library.'

'I'll work it out myself, thanks.' Rupert was almost sure he could not understand any book on aerodynamics.

By this time Selina had bought everything on her mother's list, had been pushed and elbowed along the queue until she could pay for it all, and had pushed and elbowed her own way out of the shop. Now she was taking a long way home, past all the best shop windows.

There was beautiful one in which two ladies stood tall and graceful in gold evening gowns, against a background of satiny black and purple. One lady was showing the other a sparkling necklace. Behind them stood two men in dark jackets who were smiling happy, frozen smiles. One of them held up a velvet coat for one of the ladies. Then there was a window where suntanned young men in gay polo sweaters stood petrified in careless attitudes. One had his foot on a cardboard log. Another pointed with a riding whip. All the young men stared in that direction and showed their white teeth.

Some windows had no people, but only things like typewriters or tools. Selina did not bother with those, but looked at the people in the street instead. They were better than typewriters, but not as good as the petrified people. The real people were not so smart and sleek, not as beautiful, and certainly not as gay.

There was a wonderful window with strings of dead leaves and one bare branch, a real one. It was full of young women with sparkling hair and brilliant clothes, all of them very active in a frozen way. They stood on tiptoe with flying skirts; or leant over backwards; or knelt with their arms flung out; patted large plush dogs; reached up to touch the dead branch. Selina was charmed, and stood staring at them for a long time. If only she were rich, she thought, she would rush into that shop and become as smart and happy as these young women. People—real people—jostled past her as she stood there. Someone chuckled wickedly in her ear, but when she looked there was no one there. Yet just for a moment there had been a reflection in the glass of the window: a little old man looking over her shoulder, as brown as a nut, with a long white beard.

'I'm seeing people again,' thought Selina, and she turned back to the window. But now the young women with their sparkling hair and vacant eyes looked somehow more frozen and somehow less gay. Selina's arm was suddenly aching from the weight of her mother's shopping. She forced her way back into the moving crowd, using her loaded bag as a fender or cow-catcher, and went on her way home. As she went, the city began pouring people away in buses, trains and cars like a giant pouring split peas into a jar and clapping the lid on. The Saturday-morning shopping was over.

Selina arrived at the front of the Department from one direction just as Rupert and Benny were waiting to cross with the lights from another direction. She saw them and waited, resting her bag on the pavement and gazing up at the stone walls above. When they arrived she was hopping impatiently, crying, 'Rupert, look—look!' Rupert looked up at the wall where she was pointing. A little black shape lay along the edge of a stone, near a crack. 'It's Skit!' cried Selina.

'It can't be,' said Rupert. 'It must be,' he added for the little shape lay like a fine black leaf in the very place where Skit used to lie. Selina looked up at the great white eagle across the street.

'I wonder who that was?' she said.

'Someone else in his family,' said Rupert, and added gloomily, 'It doesn't make much difference—they'll get Skit too in the end.'

'It means you've still got a lizard, anyway,' said Selina. 'Is that your book Benny's got?'

Benny turned rusty again.

'Not mine,' said Rupert. 'They only had rubbish. That's some great secret Benny got hold of.'

'See you,' said Benny soberly, and went away with his parcel.

Selina called after him, 'See you later, Benny,' and rounded on Rupert. 'You were horrible to Benny,' she declared.

'Rot,' said Rupert. In his embarrassment he picked up the bag of groceries and carried it inside.

By now he was both indignant and curious about Benny's secret. He felt badly treated, but certain that Benny would have the decency to explain in the end. He thought Benny would probably explain after lunch, if Rupert gave him the chance; so after lunch he set off for the magic shop, telling Selina that he and Benny were busy and didn't want her getting in their way. This made Selina so hurt and angry that she flew off to the Gardens by herself, promising not to speak to Rupert again.

The Potters hardly ever went to the Gardens on Saturday or Sunday. They were there every afternoon after school, when the place was so quiet that it seemed to belong to them. At the week-end there were a lot of people in the Gardens—and no one else at all in the Department or the magic shop. The week-ends were for staying at home, or going somewhere different for a change. Today Selina went to the Gardens only to show how lonely and miserable she was.

There were families with picnic lunches everywhere, and a crowd of seagulls and pigeons at every picnic.

Even the ducks came up from the pond and waddled from group to group, waiting to be fed. Small children plodded earnestly after the ducks, hoping to catch them. The ducks flapped and dodged with a good deal of noise but no panic. Young people lay on the grass and listened to radios. Older people sat on every bench in the winter sun. Selina could not even search the big rock again for her cat; a hairy young man was sitting on it, gazing out to sea as the cat had done. She was already sorry she had come. It was lonelier here, among all these strange people, than it would have been at home without Rupert or Benny.

She lingered by the pond for a while, watching the children there. A very little boy with a long piece of string pounded at his father's knee and shouted 'Fishing, Dad! I want to catch a fish!' His father tied a gold bottle-top to the end of the string, and the little boy ran back to the pond to drop his bait in the water. Selina thought he would get a shock if one of the big eels grabbed the bottle-top, so she stayed to watch.

All at once the string did jerk in the little boy's hand. He went red with excitement and began to haul it in. It could not have been an eel that tugged, Selina knew, or it would have been the little boy who was hauled in; all the same, there was some weight on the string. It came out of the water, slimy and dripping: the bottle-top had gone, and the string was neatly knotted round a small bundle of weeds. The little boy looked at it uncertainly, and trotted off to show his father. Selina dodged away at once. She did not want to be there, one child without her parents, when the father decided that someone had played a teasing trick on his little boy.

In the pond, a Pot-Koorok chuckled in a bubbling way. It was the first time for nearly two hundred years that it had been able to play one of its tricks on a fisherman. The white men fished in the harbour, and the tribes no longer fished on this coast at all. It had been a long, lonely time for the Pot-Koorok.

Selina went down to the sea-wall to look for jellyfish; but there a rowdy group of boys was running down the grassy slope and across the path, leaping at the wall. There was so much running backwards and forwards, so much leaping and shouting, that you could hardly say how many boys were there; but Selina had an impression that several of them were a dark nut-brown in colour. She moved a little away, afraid of being knocked down, and found herself beside a large, friendly dog who was watching the game too.

Selina was delighted. There were notices here and there about the Gardens that clearly said dogs were not allowed. She had never seen one in the Gardens before, and she was sure no one would have brought this dog here. It must have come uninvited through the gates from the Domain, and so far none of the gardeners had seen it. It was just the sort of company she needed—friendly and happy, with a wide grin and a lolling tongue, yet not the boisterous kind who would fling itself into a game with the boys just because of the noise they made. It had a wavy brown coat, old-looking brown eyes, and a tail that was heavily fringed and looped round towards its back.

'Good boy,' said Selina, to open the conversation. The dog turned its eyes towards her and waved its tail a little. Evidently it accepted Selina without seeing any need to make a fuss about it. She offered it her hand, which it sniffed politely before turning back to the boys.

'Nice dog,' said Selina, and moved close beside it. At this the dog leaned heavily and comfortably against her leg. Selina happily braced herself to support its weight and ventured to rub its ears. The dog rolled its eyes upward gratefully.

'You wouldn't chase my cat, would you, boy?' said Selina. The dog unlooped its tail, thumped it on the grass, and looped it back. 'Have you seen my cat, boy?' Selina went on. 'Do you know where it lives?'

The dog turned its head and looked up as if it were about to speak. Then it seemed to change its mind, and returned its ear to Selina's hand. She went on rubbing. She did not see, among the group of boys, a nut-brown face watching with a knowing smile.

The Bitarr was smiling at Selina's narrow escape. Its memory went back more than a thousand years. It knew that, in Australia, if you hear a dog talk you will turn into stone. The Bitarr loved to play with children; but stone is stone. Through the twilights and starlights of a thousand years, the Bitarr might have loved a stone shaped like Selina.

She stayed with the dog, rubbing its ears or resting her hand on the warm curve between them, until voices shouted from the lawns above—'Vernon!' 'Robert!'— and the boys swept away like a flock of pigeons. Then the dog stood up stiffly, saluted her with its tail, and went slowly back to the Domain. Selina heard the quietness of the Gardens, and felt the cold where the dog's warm coat had been. The sun was low, and all the people were going home.

The hairy young man was no longer sitting on the rock. Instead, Selina's cat was sitting there—gazing over the harbour, as it had before.

Since Selina was down near the sea-wall, the big rock rose steeply above like a small cliff. She stayed perfectly still, looking up at the cat, hoping this time to see what it did. The cat, too, stayed perfectly still for some time. Then it lowered itself over the edge of the rock, spreading its claws on the rough sandstone to grip, keeping its hind paws on the rock above while it stretched its body over the side, till it found some tiny ledge that Selina could not see. Then, with a twist and a scrabble, it disappeared before her eyes.

Keeping her eyes on the spot, Selina crept towards the stone. There was a narrow slit, hidden behind the root of a tree that curled down from above. It was high above Selina's head, so she went up the bank to the top of the rock and leaned over from above. She could see nothing—but now she knew the cat was there. She hung over the edge, head down, until her ears sang; and then she heard another sound through the singing in her ears. She held her breath and listened harder. It was still there, like the squeaking of small rusty hinges.

'Kittens!' breathed Selina.

Little electric shocks were jumping along her legs. She had never imagined kittens. She stayed there until the setting sun turned her dark hair red, and a man who was going to lock the Victoria Lodge gates called out to her. Then she scrambled up and began to run home.

She thought that Rupert would surely be back from Benny's place by now. Would she tell him straight away that her cat had kittens? Or would it be better to wait till the next time he wanted to go off with Benny and leave her at home? Selina thought she might wait for a day or so, anyway; if she could.

She came running up the little wooden stairs to the roof of the Department, banging the door behind her— and there was Rupert, at the top of the steps outside the kitchen door. He turned round and waved an urgent hand for her to be quiet. He was listening to something.

Selina stopped running and came quietly up beside him. 'What is it?' she whispered.

'Can't you hear?' hissed Rupert. 'That man's here. The one with the beard. He's asking Mum and Dad something about us.'

Chapter 6

Rupert had, in fact, been home from Benny's for hours, even more puzzled and indignant than when he went.

The magic shop had been closed, of course, so he had gone down the narrow alley at the side of the building and in at the courtyard gate. Some of Benny's school shirts had been flapping from the clothes-hoist, turning slowly round the central pole like upside-down dancers. Mr Golightly, in older clothes than he wore in the shop, had been dealing with the mats from the storeroom. He had stopped, with the broom in one knuckly hand, and said 'Rupert' in tones of uncertain welcome. When Rupert asked for Benny, Mr Golightly said, 'He's tidying his room. You won't hold him up too much, will you, Rupert? No, of course you won't, he must get that room done.' With this permission, Rupert had gone bounding up the stairs yelling, 'Hey, Benny!'

He had found Benny sitting on his unmade bed looking a little dazed and a little startled. A book lay open on his knees, but he closed it quite quickly. Rupert, looking hard, had only time to see yellow pages, brown-spotted; a diagram that seemed to be made of triangles fitted together; and a few signs that looked like letters—but not exactly like letters. Benny had pushed the book quickly into his bookshelf and said nothing at all about it.

Rupert had asked for advice about the winding gear for his wing-tips. Benny had considered, and had then replied, 'Try it out with string and see.' Rupert had asked for help. Benny had said, 'I've got to tidy this room.' Rupert had asked if he would come round tomorrow, and Benny had said, 'If I can. I'll see.' Rupert had waited a little, giving Benny time to explain things. Benny had not explained them.

'What about that wonderful book you bought today?' Rupert had asked at last. 'Any good?'

'Don't know yet,' said Benny, pink and sober. 'I said I'd tell you when I know.'

So Rupert had gone home again in disgust, to work

on his plane for the afternoon without even Selina there. He could not even show his disgust by flinging off to the Gardens, for there was no one to see him go. He tangled the string of the winding gear, and had to spend a long time untangling it. Then he made a hole in the brown-paper covering of the wings. He was patching this angrily when he heard the door on to the roof open, and his father come through with someone else. There were his father's heavy, slow footsteps, and the voice of a man who was with him.

'. . . quite an opportunity for the children, you know,' the man was saying. 'It might lead to something quite big, as I'm sure you realise. Of course I expect you to check my references very thoroughly.'

'We'll just see what the wife thinks, Mr Hawke,' said Mr Potter's slow voice. 'Then we'll have to see what the kids think.'

Rupert, out of sight in the second lane, kept quite still and peeped round the corner. His father was standing at the kitchen door with the bearded man whom Selina had nearly knocked over.

'Mother,' Mr Potter was saying, 'this is Mr Hawke. He's in advertising.'

'And in Public Relations,' added Mr Hawke with a little bow. He seemed to be awed by the importance of advertising and Public Relations.

'He's got a proposition,' said Mr Potter—and at this point they all went inside. Rupert was annoyed with them. He could hear nothing more; yet it was clear from what his father had said that the proposition was something to do with him. He crept close to the kitchen door to listen. He was still there when Selina came home.

'*What* man with a beard?' whispered Selina, creeping on to the top step beside him. 'Not that one I bumped into?'

'Sh! I told you, didn't I?'

'What are they talking about?'

'About us,' said Rupert, who had not been able to hear a word since they went inside.

'Why? What have we done?'

'I don't know, clot. Can't you listen?'

Selina listened. All she could hear was several pairs of feet coming to the back door. She and Rupert rushed down the steps and were standing at the foot, breathless, when Mr Hawke came out again with their mother and father.

'Here are the children now,' said Mrs Potter, and introduced them in her usual way. 'This is my second boy Rupert. This is my girl Selina.' To the children she said, 'Mr Hawke would like you to pose for some photographs for television. For commercials.'

Rupert and Selina gaped. Mr Hawke looked hurt.

'Not *photographs*,' he protested, 'film. And I don't want you to *pose*. Just do a bit of clambering about while I film. You'd like that, wouldn't you? I know you're good at it.' He smiled at them, showing a lot of teeth among the beard. 'And then, if we were lucky, you might see yourselves on television.'

Selina adored television—but suddenly she was not sure that she wanted to see herself on it. Rupert thought television a bit slow, but he knew he would love it if he were doing the acting. He went red with excitement, while Selina stared numbly. Mr Hawke smiled again and rubbed his hands.

'The girl,' he said confidentially to Mrs Potter. 'She's the one . . . But wasn't there another one? With freckles?'

'Benny,' said Rupert quickly. 'That was Benny.'

'Rupert's friend Benny Golightly,' Mrs Potter explained. 'We can't answer for him, but Rupert can take a message to Mr Golightly.'

'Now?' said Rupert.

'Tomorrow,' said Mrs Potter, 'when we've made up our own minds.'

'Well,' said Mr Hawke, 'you'll find my references in order and you have my telephone number. I'll look forward to hearing from you.' He jerked a little in farewell and went away. Mr Potter followed, to see him safely out of the Department.

'What do we have to make up our minds about?' asked Rupert, astonished.

'A lot of things,' said Mrs Potter. 'Whether this man Hawke is the type I'd want to send you off to the Gardens with, for one . . .'

'Oh, Mum! You know it's full of gardeners and people.'

'. . . and whether we want you making a show of yourselves on commercials, for another.'

'Television!' said Selina in a squeaky voice. Her mother looked at her sharply.

'You don't have to do it,' she said. 'If the man's all right you can just please yourself, so don't let's have a performance.'

'Oh, Selina . . .' began Rupert, but his mother cut him off sharply.

'That's enough, Rupert. Selina will please herself.'

Selina still felt numb, and crept away to her room. She stayed there while her mother set the table, while

Greg came home from a football match and heard the exciting news, while her father made some telephone calls to find out about Mr Hawke. She came out only to feed her cat and Morris. Then she remembered the kittens, and felt better.

Still she could not make up her mind; and Rupert, under Mrs Potter's eye, kept a gloomy silence. For Selina, the worst time was in the evening, watching the television commercials. There were people floating through the air; children drinking cordials and saying 'M-m-m' greedily to show how nice they were; children dressing up outlandishly in their parents' clothes to prove how good somebody's starch was; children covering themselves with mud to prove how good somebody's washing powder was; children saying, with awful primness, 'My mummy *always* gives me So-and-So's cheese. It's *good*.' Rupert watched them with a small, pleased grin; but Selina knew she would die if she had to do anything like that.

It took her a long time to get to sleep that night—but in the morning she found she had made up her mind while she slept. She would do what Mr Hawke wanted, for a number of rather odd reasons. One, of course, was that Rupert wanted to do it, and Benny probably would too. Another was that she was interested in Mr Hawke, and especially the glimpse she remembered of him sitting, head down, at a table loaded with sweets. A third reason was that the filming was to be done in the Botanical Gardens at three o'clock on Monday afternoon, when the light was still good and yet there were not many people. The children would have to be excused early from school, and this had an important and exciting feel about it. The

71

last thing was that if she did not agree to do this now, Selina had a feeling she would be angry with herself in a few weeks' time.

'It's all right,' she said at breakfast, with her head down in an embarrassed way. 'I'll do it.'

'Wow!' yelled Rupert. 'Can I go and tell Benny?'

'You'll finish your breakfast,' said Mrs Potter. 'I'll write a note to Mr Golightly later.'

'Couple of stars in the family, eh?' said Greg. 'Can you lend us a fiver, mate?'

'It'll go in the Bank,' said Mrs Potter quickly, while Rupert and Selina were still looking astonished at the idea of being *paid* to appear on television. 'I don't know, I'm sure . . .' she added, appealing to Mr Potter. 'I don't know that it'll be good for them . . .'

'Bit of a nine days' wonder,' said Mr Potter comfortably, 'and we'll all have a good laugh. That's all.'

Later, Rupert and Selina went together to Benny's place, for Selina felt sufficiently like a heroine to refuse to be left behind. They took Mrs Potter's note with them, and found Mr Golightly in the sunny courtyard brooding over a sad-looking gardenia in a tub.

'Selina,' he said absently. 'Rupert . . . I don't know that I can pull it through another winter.'

They gave him the note, and then looked at each other rather hopelessly. It did not seem likely that he would understand anything so fantastic as Mr Hawke's proposition. 'You go and find Benny,' Selina advised. 'I'll stay here.' For that matter, it might not be easy to make Benny understand, either. Rupert went in search of him while Selina stayed beside Mr Golightly.

In the end, it was much simpler than she had expected.

Mr Golightly was so bewildered by the proposition that he did not attempt to understand it at all. He was not even very clear about what a commercial was, and decided in a puzzled way to put his faith in Mr and Mrs Potter. 'What they have decided for you and Rupert,' he said to Selina, 'will be best for Benny, I'm sure.' Selina had only to persuade him to write a note to Benny's teacher now, before he forgot, asking that Benny might be excused from school at a quarter to three. He did this in order to be rid of Selina, so that he could go back to his gardenia and rub some more soot off its leaves. Selina carried the note upstairs to Benny.

Rupert was having a little more trouble explaining matters to Benny. 'It's a *commercial*,' he was saying very loudly. 'We get *paid* for it. And then we come on television.' This seemed to Rupert the clearest possible explanation of every point.

'But what does he want us to *do*?' asked Benny, puzzled. 'Why did he pick on *us*?'

Selina gave him the note. 'He wants us to clamber about while he films,' she said, mentally crossing her fingers. She added, because she had been thinking about it when she could not get to sleep last night, 'I think he saw us burying that one that wasn't Skit. It was right under his window.' Benny thought this over, and Rupert took the chance to look quickly at the book lying open on the bed. There was a whole page of those signs that looked like letters, but like queer letters.

'Anyhow,' said Rupert, to clinch the argument, 'it means getting out of school early. And if you don't want to see yourself on television, I *do*.'

'Well, I don't care,' said Benny at last, 'as long as it's

only climbing something. As long as we don't have to dress up or anything crazy like that.'

'I was scared of that too,' Selina confessed. 'If he wants us to, we won't.' Suddenly she was far less nervous about the whole unlikely scheme. To have Benny coming too, puzzling over it in his worried way and determined not to do anything crazy, made it seem more real and sensible. She thought that if Benny would help, they could manage that funny Mr Hawke.

She managed to hold on to this idea all day, though it was hard when Rupert was so restless with excitement. She thought of the kittens often, and wished she could go off to see them. She wondered why she had not told Rupert and Benny about them yet, and put off the idea until after tomorrow. She told herself that Rupert was in a silly mood about the television film, and wouldn't listen properly; but there was another feeling, too. Selina wanted Rupert and Benny to know nothing about the kittens while they were in the Gardens with Ernest Hawke. 'He has funny eyes,' she thought, 'and his teeth look different in the middle of all that beard.' She was interested in him—but she didn't want to trust him with her kittens.

In the evening, Rupert watched television for as long as he was allowed to stay up; but Selina would not look at it at all. She was not going to make herself scared again, so she went to bed with a book to read. She put her light out early, and watched the pale colours flash across her room from the electric signs. She heard Rupert being sent to bed; heard Greg come from the shower and say good night; heard her mother and father shutting doors and settling down. When everything was quiet, she got up for a little while and looked out of her window. All the lights were sparkling like coloured raindrops sharp in the cold air. Selina got back into bed and went to sleep.

Everyone was asleep, on all the roof-tops. In a tiny house by the harbour, old Harry was asleep too; he was dreaming that he had kicked the polisher in a vital place and it had suddenly exploded. The shabby old man had hung up his shabby coat and was sleeping in a grey flannel shirt; he looked like a tired old rat.

The Minister was not asleep. He was sitting at home, in a deep chair, with a book that he was not reading. He was thinking of the people, who wanted money more than they wanted their Gardens. He wondered what they would buy with it: more Gardens, perhaps.

Sir Mortimer Wyvern was not asleep, either. He was listening to music; but sometimes his mind would come up from the music like a clock suddenly striking. He must see his new building soon—the parking space underneath was a good idea . . . There was that meeting of important men on Tuesday—they would settle the plan for the Gardens then . . . The music washed over him again.

Neither was Benny asleep yet. He had gone to bed early, but had taken down the old book he had found in the second-hand bookshop. He was still puzzling over strange signs and mysterious, unreadable letters. 'A sign to control evil spirits,' he read; and, 'To render the magician invisible.' Benny shivered a little and turned the brittle pages. Somewhere there might be a small, harmless charm for a beginner to try . . . 'To call a toad to your hand;' now, that was the sort of thing he had in mind. He read on, trying to make out the old words, until Mr

Golightly called to him to go to sleep at once and put the light out.

The city hummed and grumbled, never sleeping. It whispered in the splashing of its fountains and breathed in the tides of its harbour. It spread its net of lights to shut out the stars, and held the land in a grip of concrete and steel. Yet deep under the city, forgotten under the concrete, the land was still there.

Its soil was there, stripped of ferns and shut away forever from the sun. Its stone was there, deep and abiding; and out of the stone the Nyols crept, the old creatures of the land. They found their way up through tunnels and drains, and slithered through gratings into the darkest places. The lights did not please them, for they liked their lights to be far and pale, and lit by distant suns. They found the city a harsh, dead place; but still they came to feel the wind.

In the Gardens, the Pot-Koorok climbed out of the pond. It was still chuckling and bubbling over the trick it had played on the little boy—the first for two hundred years. It left wet foot prints on the edge of the pond; like a frog's but much bigger.

In the darkness very far away, Greg's comet was coming closer.

Chapter 7

On the morning of that Monday when Rupert, Selina and Benny were to be captured on film for television, Sir Mortimer Wyvern began a busy day. Ash, his driver, was having a day off to visit the dentist, and Sir Mortimer drove his own shiny, important car to town. There was no Lady Wyvern to wave him goodbye, and no little Wyverns either. There was only Mrs Ash, who kept house for him.

As the very top man of Commerce, Sir Mortimer had a great many friends. He worked hard at making and keeping important friends because they were often useful to him in business. For the same reason, lesser men of Commerce worked hard at making a friend of Sir Mortimer. He was not at all a lonely man, but he had never had time for a wife and family. 'Commerce is my wife and family,' he would sometimes say to the lesser men; and then he would sigh a little, pretending that it was his duty to be sad and lonely because of all the people who depended on him.

So there was only Mrs Ash, the wife of his driver. 'I shall be home quite early,' Sir Mortimer told her. 'I want to see Brown, and one or two other people, about a very important meeting tomorrow night.'

Brown was his secretary. In his shiny, important office, Sir Mortimer talked to Brown about the meeting. It was the meeting at which he would launch his plan for building a car-park in the Botanical Gardens. He was sure there was no better way to serve Commerce and the city; and, though he knew the Minister would fight against the plan, he did not think the Minister would fight very hard. He would know he was beaten already, for Sir Mortimer would have persuaded all the important men who would be at the meeting.

Sir Mortimer spoke to some of them on the telephone again, to make sure. 'I will suggest the plan myself at the right moment,' he reminded each one. 'I shall count on your disinterested view of the serious nature of the problem—and of course your support when I make my suggestion . . . The Minister? I don't think we need worry unduly. He will have to make a show, of course; but I can claim to have treated him very fairly . . . I have also prevented him from making anything public too soon . . . I shall see you at eight-thirty, then. And thank you, George.' (Or Edward, or Bill.) 'I'm glad to have your help. You must call on mine some time.' And Edward, Bill or George made a mental note that he certainly would.

Then Sir Mortimer arranged to meet the Mayor of the city by accident and take him to lunch. He wanted to point out to the Mayor that unless something were done about squeezing more cars into the city, several very important businesses would move out of the city altogether. 'The situation is very grave, Tom,' he said, shaking his head. 'I'm afraid the city must suffer unless something can be done.'

After lunch he talked to the editor of his newspaper, to tell him what the news would be on Wednesday morning and how the paper must explain it to the people. Then he thought he would have a look at his new building, where the ground level was being opened up for parking cars. He thought the Minister might say, 'If Commerce needs more parking space, Commerce should provide it.' Then Sir Mortimer would be ready for him: 'The whole of this space will provide parking for only eighty cars. It is a drop in the ocean, gentlemen, but what more can I do?' But first he would look at the space for himself, although he had seen the plans. It was because he always made sure of these things for himself that Sir Mortimer was the top man of Commerce.

He went back to his car and drove to Arrow Place,

where the building stood. He thought it would take him five minutes to see the place; then he would drive home, two hours before the evening rush began.

Arrow Place was one of those quiet little places where the crowds never came. There was a narrow little pavement, and a wall of strong wooden hoardings, and rising above them Sir Mortimer's building in a cage of steel. He had bought it cheaply because it was old, and now he was making it into something modern and huge. High overhead a great machine was working, singing over and over two giant, dreamy notes. Behind the hoardings a pneumatic drill chattered and shrieked, breaking up stone and old concrete for the new parking space.

Sir Mortimer parked his car and locked it. Then he walked to an opening in the hoardings and looked into a wide and shadowy space. The workmen saw his thin, neat figure and smooth, narrow face, and they nudged one another. They knew who he was. The shrieking of the drill stopped, and the men went quietly away to find the foreman. It would not be tactful to rend the ears of the Owner with the noise of a pneumatic drill. They left the dim space behind the hoardings to Sir Mortimer.

He smiled a little. He liked the importance and noise of pneumatic drills, for they were usually doing the work of Commerce; but he liked it, too, when they stopped respectfully for him. He walked in among the rubble, stepping neatly and carefully in his polished shoes. He stepped on to the broken stone—and stumbled a little. Something had grabbed his foot; something had pulled.

Sir Mortimer teetered and waved his arms. The loosened stone rumbled a little. He bent down to grab his own ankle, and the stone heaved gently. His second ankle was being pulled too. Sir Mortimer thought perhaps he had better yell for help.

'Ho, there!' he cried; but his throat had forgotten how to make a good, full-sized shout. The huge machine working above changed from its lower to its higher note and covered the sound. Struggling wildly and calling 'Ho, there! Ho!' Sir Mortimer Wyvern was pulled down into some secret, hidden chasm in the rock. There was no sign left except his car, parked outside the hoardings.

Just at this time Benny, Rupert and Selina were coming slowly towards the kiosk in the Gardens to meet Mr Ernest Hawke. They had all changed from school clothes into old jeans, as they had been told, and they were all nervous; even Rupert, now that the time had come. Selina stayed behind the two boys, but close behind.

They could see Mr Hawke, with a portable movie camera and a bag, his strange eyes watching everything. He looked round and found their three pairs of eyes examining him, giving nothing away. They did not speak; he could see that they were waiting to listen. He spoke briskly.

'Ice-cream or chocolate?'

There was a flicker in each pair of eyes. They all said, 'Ice-cream.'

Ernest Hawke bought four ice-creams and led the way to a bench near by. The good light would not last long; he could spare just a minute or two for coaxing his nervous subjects to relax. He handed out ice-creams.

'Spread it around a bit, all right? We don't want those faces too clean. You know what you're doing this afternoon, don't you? You're helping me work some magic.'

They said nothing, but they looked alert and interested,

ready to laugh when the joke came.

'You've heard of witches and wizards and magicians, who used to work magic once?' They all nodded. Benny stopped licking. 'You think they did it with charms and magic ointment?' They nodded again. 'Garbage,' said Ernest Hawke calmly. 'They worked magic in the only real way: with people's minds. Magicians and all that lot—they were just people who could make other people believe things. They used other people's minds for their own good. I'm a modern magician, and you're going to help me.'

He opened his bag and took out some bars wrapped in red and silver foil. 'You and I,' he said, 'are going to make every man, woman and child in the country believe they want to eat Crackle-Crunch, all right? They all know they'd really rather have money in the bank, and nice slim waists, and good teeth—but we're going to make them believe that most of all they want to eat Crackle-Crunch.'

'Why?' said Selina.

Mr Hawke leaned forward and grinned so that all the white teeth showed in his beard. 'Ha!' he said. 'Little Miss Potter. You think I'm going to say for their own good, don't you? So that everyone can get a job making Crackle-Crunch, and the money keeps going round? Garbage. That's just another charm for using people's minds. We're doing it because J. H. Treacle and Co, who make this product, are paying us good money to do it. For our own good, Miss Potter, all right?'

The eyes were looking at him with doubt and reserve. He thought they were probably too young to understand his clever argument; but they were not looking stiff and

82

nervous any more. Selina asked, 'Do we have to say anything?'

'Not a word,' said Ernest Hawke, looking at his watch and checking the light. 'You've just got to climb a few places I've picked out—I've got permission, for just this once—and when you get to the top you'll take a Crackle-Crunch out of your pocket, or your sleeve or somewhere, and hold it up and pretend you found it there. The slogan is "They'll go anywhere for Crackle-Crunch". Got the idea? Easy, isn't it?'

It really was very easy. All the places Ernest Hawke had picked for them to climb were very easy places, with no danger at all of falling. Often he could put the bars of Crackle-Crunch in position first, so that there was no trouble about carrying them up. They had to climb on the lions by the old stone wall and reach up high to 'find' the Crackle-Crunch among the ivy. There was a good low tree just outside the gates in the Domain; they all climbed easily into that and waved the red-and-silver bars from among its leaves. They climbed rocks and gates, and down the banks of the little stream under one of the bridges. They easily forgot the camera because Ernest Hawke was good at keeping it out of sight, and because he talked all the time about the modern magic of advertising, or what he called Public Relations. Selina asked what they were, because they sounded like a large public family; but Ernest Hawke explained gravely that they were the greatest power in the world today, and a way of making people think what you wanted them to think. Selina continued to find him interesting, but less and less someone to like. He, on the other hand, seemed to like her. He liked Benny too, but seemed to take less notice of Rupert. This was a little odd, because Rupert was the one who liked Mr Hawke and really enjoyed being filmed. The trouble was that he enjoyed it a little too much.

Selina was good; she climbed so quickly and waved her Crackle-Crunch with such a triumphant grin. Benny was good too. He had a way of looking at his Crackle-Crunch with a thoughtful surprise that delighted Mr Hawke. Rupert was inclined to clown a little, and had to be pulled up once or twice. But on the whole it was all so quick and successful that Mr Hawke was very pleased with them.

He did not even mind when a demonstration came marching down Macquarie Street and the children raced away from Governor Phillip's fountain to watch Ernest Hawke simply followed them to the fence and stood behind them while they watched the people shouting and waving their banners. Not until the shouts became angry did he call them away.

'Come on, then—one more climb and you've earned another ice-cream. This is the wrong sort of Public Relations for us. It won't do any good.'

'Why won't it?' Selina demanded in a prickly voice.

He grinned at her. 'Miss Y. Potter. It won't do any good because it's so unintelligent. You can't force a lot of people to do what a few people want; you only put yourself in the wrong by trying. And when you've only got a few people, you shouldn't gather them all together in one place—it gives the others a chance to count them. And if you've only got a small force to use against a big one, you shouldn't wait until the big force has rolled into position and settled down before you try to shift it;

84

you should attack quickly, while things are still moving, before they're settled. That's if you really want to produce anything but a bit of fun and a row . . . Up on that railing with you, now.'

'Anyhow, they're trying,' said Selina resentfully as she and the boys climbed on to the railing of the bandstand. She still believed in the demonstrators.

'Very trying,' Ernest Hawke agreed, aiming the camera.

'Selina thinks they're wonderful,' scoffed Rupert, putting himself on Mr Hawke's side.

Selina's climb on the bandstand was her worst of the day, for something else had come into her mind. When it was over—when Ernest Hawke had told them to keep their Crackle-Crunch and to come to the kiosk for another ice-cream—she looked at him sideways and spoke rather carefully.

'What if someone *was* going to do something? Like in the Gardens; say they wanted to build a road or something . . .'

'*Selina*,' hissed Rupert; and Benny looked bothered. Mr Hawke's peculiar eyes passed over them, trotting along beside him to keep pace with his long strides.

'Car-park *and* entrance road,' he said briefly. 'Through the Domain. It's all settled. Nothing to be done about it.'

They were staring at him. 'But it's a secret!' cried Selina, scandalised. 'Anyhow, I don't believe you. The Minister wouldn't let them.'

'He won't be able to help it. The meeting's tomorrow night at eight-thirty, in the Party Rooms behind Parliament House. It's settled already.'

'How do *you* know?'

'I know a journalist on the *Star* newspaper. Had a late

85

lunch with him today. Sir Mortimer Wyvern owns the *Star*.'

'Of course he knows, Selina, you nut,' said Rupert quickly.

They were almost at the kiosk. 'Couldn't you stop it?' said Selina, accusing him. 'If your magic Relations are so wonderful?'

He grinned at her. 'Nobody's paying me,' said Ernest Hawke.

Selina was both shocked and angry. She took the ice-cream he gave her because she did not know how to refuse it; but she hoped she had taken it in an insulting way, and she did not even take the lid off the little cardboard bucket. Nor did she speak to Mr Hawke again, even to say 'thank you'.

He grinned at her stiff back as though he still liked her, and went away.

'Selina, you clot,' said Rupert crossly.

She whirled on him. 'I don't care! And you needn't wait for me, I'm going home by myself, so there!' She ran away past the pond towards Farm Cove.

'She's got no sense,' said Rupert roundly. 'And she's left her schoolcase for me to carry, too. She can just go home by herself; and if Mum wants to know why, I'll just tell her, that's all.'

Selina went running down to the big rock where the kittens were. She needed the kittens after all the upsetting afternoon; and she thought that a good thing to do with Ernest Hawke's ice-cream would be to give it to the cat. When she reached the rock she lay flat on the top of it and leaned over the edge. A low growl came from inside the rock: the cat was at home.

Selina did not think it would scratch her, after all the weeks of feeding. She took the lid off the ice-cream bucket and pushed it into the cleft with her bare hand. Then she lay still and listened. She thought she could hear the cat lapping at the ice-cream, but she was not really sure. The kittens were so quiet that she wondered if they were still there. She lay listening for a long time, trying to be sure, while the sun went low down the sky and lit her dark hair with red. After a while she reached into the cleft again and took out the ice-cream bucket. It was empty.

Rather nervously, but not able to help it, she put her hand into the cleft again. At once she heard the cat growl. She did not pull her hand out, though it wanted to come of itself, but let it stay while she waited again. When nothing had happened for some time, she pushed it in a little further.

She lay still while the sun set, and the red light faded from her hair, and the city howled. A man came to lock the gates, but she was lying so still that he did not see her or call to her. Selina did not see the man, either, for her eyes were fixed on the ground below. Inside the rock, something very soft had just squirmed against her hand.

She lay there, hardly breathing, while the small soft thing bobbed and squirmed against her hand. A man came walking, head down, on the grass below the rock: not a gardener, but a broad, fair man in a very neat grey suit. Selina hardly knew he was there, and certainly did not realise that both he and she had been locked into the Gardens. The soft little thing inside the rock was fumbling its way into her hand. Very gently she closed her hand about it and drew it out. It mewed in a shrill and penetrating voice.

It was tiny and purplish grey and blind. It turned its round head blindly from side to side, squealing, and the ears looked even too small for the head. Selina was full of delight. She held the kitten down towards the man, who was now looking up at her.

'See?' she said.

Then she saw that the man was the Minister.

Chapter 8

The Minister had been in the Gardens for some time. He had come there, as he often did when he was worried, to think about the meeting tomorrow night. He knew that Sir Mortimer Wyvern would already have talked about his plan to all the important men who would be at the meeting. He was sure they would decide to build a very large car-park in the Botanical Gardens as soon as possible, though he meant to fight against it as well as he could. He had all his arguments ready—but he had come here looking for hope and belief, thinking he might find them if he could see the people enjoying their Gardens.

On a Monday afternoon in winter, he found, there were very few people here. One or two old men sat on benches in the late sun; a tourist or two took photographs of the fountains; some children climbed on the band-stand; an old man drifted from one garbage-bin to the next. No one looked at the pink of the silk-floss flowers against the sky. No one gazed at the golden lamps on the yellow-wood tree. No one watched the pale, clear water moving against the sea-wall. The Minister wondered if he were mistaken; perhaps no one wanted the Gardens after all.

He stood and looked over the harbour at the lovely and terrible city. He sat on the grass near a patch of shrubs and watched the sun setting, without thinking at all about the gates being locked; and because he sat so still behind the shrubs, the men who locked them did not notice him. He had still not thought about the gates when he stood up again, and strolled under the high rocks. He heard a shrill crying and looked up at the rocks; and up there, a little girl's face was looking down at him.

'See?' she said, and held down a kitten, very small and young. It mewed in the tiny but penetrating voice of all small kittens.

The Minister could see a pair of sullen yellow eyes glowing from the dark slit in the rock. 'Careful,' he warned. 'Its mother might scratch you.'

'I don't think she will,' said Selina. 'I feed her every night. . . Do you want to hold it?'

The Minister reached up and took the kitten carefully. Selina pulled her sweater sleeve right down over her hand and waited, giving him a chance to have a proper nurse. The kitten attached itself to his grey suit, and she giggled while he unhooked it. He was smiling when he handed it back. Selina placed it carefully in the wool-covered hand, gripping kitten and turned-over sleeve together. Very gently she returned it to the rock, while the Minister stood holding his breath. He expected to have to leap to her rescue and untangle a fighting cat from the woollen sweater.

'It's all right,' said Selina. 'I think she does know me. You wouldn't think there were kittens in there, would you?'

'Isn't it late for you to be here?' asked the Minister; for he suddenly saw the grey-blue twilight, and the cold grey water, and the sparkle of city lights beyond. Selina giggled again.

'We're both locked in,' she told him. 'It doesn't matter, we can get out through the top fence. Do you know that way?'

The Minister shook his head. 'But we needn't do that, you know. We can go out through the Government House gates.'

Selina stared at him. 'But they don't like it if you get locked in,' she pointed out. 'And the loose bit of fence is just here. I can show you.'

'Splendid!' said the Minister bravely. He felt suddenly light of heart, and almost wanted to apologise for his dull idea about the Government House gates. And now

91

he believed with all his heart that a car-park in the Gardens was a ridiculous idea.

'You come up some steps just there,' said Selina, pointing.

'I know them,' said the Minister. He moved out of the fading light, into the deeper twilight of the bank. There seemed to be a fluttering of small shadows, all about the rocks and shrubs, and sidling past him on the steps. The wind in the leaves and the wash of the sea made a distant chuckling, and a far-away sighing. Selina stood waiting at the top of the steps; and behind her, surely, a small grey hairy person with claws? The Minister gave a surprised little laugh.

Selina looked at him gravely. 'I see things here, too,' she said. Then she added something that popped out by itself, surprising her very much. 'I suppose they have to go somewhere.'

'I suppose so,' said the Minister. He remembered Sir Mortimer Wyvern and the brown children with beards, and smiled to himself again. 'Though I believe they get around a little. Perhaps it was one of them who took my ivory paper-knife. A pity. I miss that knife.'

Selina stood still for a second, feeling hot and squeezed. 'Ivory?' she said with a squeak.

'Elephants' tusks, you know. Mine came from China and was quite an antique. I expect I've just mislaid it, and it will turn up.'

'*I didn't know, I'll put it back, I'll put it back,*' Selina's mind was gabbling. Then something scuttled by in the twilight, and she found she had grabbed the Minister's hand. He held hers in a firm and steadying way, so that she was able to tell herself that of course she would put the knife back, she had always meant to, and anyway he had probably not said that at all.

They followed a path along the inside of the fence, between tall shrubs that made it very shadowy indeed. The Minister did not mind, for he knew it would be better if no one saw him crawling out of the Botanical Gardens in an unlawful way. It was part of his duty to be dignified and correct on behalf of his government. All the same, he had made up his mind not to disgrace Selina whatever happened. He would not flinch or shuffle even if Sir Mortimer himself were waiting outside the fence. A fig for Sir Mortimer. A fig for the Premier, even. If the Minister were going to break out of the Gardens he would do it with coolness and spirit, like the child herself.

'Forward,' he said firmly, still leading her by the hand. 'And let there be no moaning of the bars,' he commanded.

Selina giggled. Behind them the Net-Net, the small hairy person with claws, was peering with bright, dark eyes into the cat's hole. Fierce golden eyes glared back, and the cat growled. The Net-Net scampered back up the rock. Farther off, the Pot-Koorok came to the surface of the pond and blew a few bubbles.

Selina led the Minister off the path, right in among the dark shrubs. 'This is the best place,' she said, grasping two iron rods of the fence. They looked as though they were firmly set in concrete, but in fact they had rusted through at the base. Selina pushed them apart quite easily. Then she glanced thoughtfully at the Minister and pushed aside the next two bars as well, to make a wider space. 'Can you get through there?' she asked him.

'Certainly I can,' said the Minister, a little hurt. A fig

93

for the Permanent Secretary too! 'What's that?' he asked suddenly, catching sight of a white figure hidden among the shrubs.

'It's all right,' Selina told him, 'it's just "Summer". She's a lovely lady—white stone—with all wheat and stuff—only I don't think the gardeners like her. They keep her right in here, and you can't even see her unless you crawl in.'

The Minister crouched and edged himself through the space between the bars. He did flinch a little, but only to keep his grey suit away from the rust; and once he was through he stood up straight and looked about with great coolness. No one was in sight in all this part of the Domain; not even the Permanent Secretary. Selina skipped through after him and straightened the bars so that they sat back on their rusted ends again.

They stood on the narrow path in the Domain and smiled at each other. Then Selina said 'Goodbye' rather quickly and shyly, and began to back away from him along the path in the shadow of the Gardens.

'Wait!' called the Minister. 'It's late—I must see you home safely.'

'I have to go,' gabbled Selina, and turned and ran. She had remembered that she had his ivory paper-knife under the lining of her drawer, and had almost been caught in his office, and was going to get into trouble for being so late. She could never let him take her home to the Department!

'Come back, child!' he called, hurrying after her. 'You mustn't go off by yourself!' But she was already gone, into the twilight. The Minister wondered who this child was that he had met in the Gardens, with a kitten in her hand

94

and a hairy little person standing behind. He was only more certain than ever that the Gardens was no place for a car-park.

Selina was almost home by now, still running hard. 'I was with the Minister,' she panted, trying out the injured way she would say it to her mother. She could hardly wait to tell Rupert about him, and the kittens and everything.

Rupert was already in disgrace for having come home without her. Selina was in disgrace too, the moment she came slinking on to the roof.

'I thought you had more sense, Selina, staying out till after dark by yourself. I knew this television rubbish would go to your head. I shouldn't have let you do it.'

'But I wasn't by myself!' cried Selina, in just the right injured tone. 'I thought it was all right if I was with the Minister!'

Her mother was too angry to take any notice of this unusual story. 'You were wrong, then. It's never all right unless your father and I know where you are. You know that quite well. Now here we are, supposed to be going to play cards with Mr and Mrs Young tomorrow night, and how do I know what you'll get up to when my back's turned? I thought I could trust you. I've a good mind not to go.'

That stung. 'I'll be in bed before you go,' said Selina, really injured this time. 'Greg will be here.'

'It's not a thing I like to ask of Greg when you go on like this. I'll have to see what he thinks about it.'

She did ask Greg, too; for Mrs Potter was really angry, and determined that Rupert and Selina should know it. Greg listened patiently and said, 'They'll be right. I'll

95

tie them up.' Mr Potter, happening to come into the kitchen, added that if they were not all right he would deal with them when he got home. Mrs Potter decided that the matter had now been settled, and allowed it to drop.

'Tomorrow night . . .' Greg was gazing at nothing in a dreamy way. 'That's when the comet comes . . .' His family did not break into his thoughts; they all knew what the comet meant to Greg.

Rupert followed Selina out to feed the cat, which came in its usual mysterious way in spite of the ice-cream.

' "I was with the Minister",' Rupert jeered. 'Couldn't you think up anything better than that? You wouldn't know him if you saw him.'

'I do so know him, I've seen him four times. He got out through the fence with me. And he nursed one of my kittens.'

'Kittens? What are you talking about?'

Selina had the pleasure of telling him all about it, and Rupert listened with envy and horror. For a time he did not know what to say; but in the end he said, 'Selina, you nut!' and they both giggled for some time.

During dinner they were allowed to come out of disgrace and tell their mother and father about the television filming. Greg was there too, of course, but they knew he was not listening. He still had the dreamy look on his face. Rupert did most of the talking. Mr Potter listened carefully and kept nodding in an interested way. Mrs Potter asked a lot of questions, and did not call the film 'that television rubbish' again.

Later, in bed, Selina remembered the Minister's paper-knife, not plastic but ivory. It made her feel hot and prickly, and she began to wonder when she could take it back to his room. She was determined that Rupert should not know anything about the knife—no one should know, but especially not Rupert—but it would be hard to put it back without his knowing. Then she remembered that tomorrow night her parents would be out. Greg would be dreamy about his comet, and would hardly notice anything else. She might go quietly down to the Minister's room and be back in just a few minutes. She would only have to dodge Rupert.

Greg was sure to stay on the roof, looking at the sky; so she could not go that way. She would go by the little staircase they hardly ever used, the one outside the living-room that was used when visitors came and Mrs Potter wanted to bring them in by her front door . . . Selina was not frightened of the dark, she knew where all the switches were, and anyway there was always a lot of light coming in from the street . . . She would get rid of the awful knife, and come back and see the comet . . . like a great sky-rocket . . . streaking across the sky . . . Selina was asleep.

Rupert was asleep, too; but Benny was rooting in the garbage-can just outside the door of Mr Golightly's store room.

He was looking for the claw of a chicken that his father had cooked for dinner. The legs had come frozen in the pack with the chicken, in case you wanted to make chicken broth; but Mr Golightly had felt that he could easily bear to waste this opportunity and had simply thrown away the chicken's legs and the little parcel of giblets. Benny needed a leg for his spell to call up a toad, and had waited till his father was busy taking stock to

97

creep out to the courtyard and look for it. He had collected everything else the spell needed, or things as near to them as he could get. The chicken's leg was as near as he could get to a ground-pigeon's claw; he would not have wanted to get any nearer, even if there had been ground-pigeons nesting in Pitt Street.

In approaching the spells in the old book Benny's mind had wavered uncertainly, almost from the moment when he found the book under an untidy heap on a table in the bookshop. He longed to prove that a spell could work—a real spell, not just stage-magic. Yet he had a shivery, distrustful feeling about all the spells he had read. Reading them had been hard work, too, because of the old words and the funny way they were used. When he could manage to work them out, he hardly knew what half the things were that the recipes needed—and he hated the idea of a lot of those that he did know. But he thought the spell to call up a toad could hardly do any harm to anyone; and it seemed to become his special spell when he found that he already had one of the most difficult things to put in it. 'The slough of an adder', he had read. When he worked it out with the dictionary, that became 'a snake's cast-off skin'. Benny had one of those, soft and rustly and dry, almost transparent yet still surprisingly strong. He had found it two years ago on a holiday in the country, and had kept it ever since in a tobacco tin. What better way could you use such a thing than by making a spell to call up a toad?

He unwrapped one more bundle of orange-skins, tea-leaves and egg-shells, and poked about in it with a stick. Here was the chicken's leg at last. He pushed it aside while he rewrapped the parcel and put the lid back on the bin. Then he took it to the kitchen sink and washed it. It was white and scale-marked like the adder's slough. He wondered whether he should cut off the foot with its curled-up claws, and decided that as long as he had the claws it did not matter that they were still attached to the leg. He took the leg to his bedroom and laid out all his collection on the dressing-table. Then he took down the old book and read the charm again:

TO CALL A TOAD TO YOUR HAND

Take bladder-wort and place it in a vessel with leaves of the nightshade. Put with it also claws of the ground-pigeon tied about with the slough of the adder. Having poured on water, put the vessel to the fire till it boil. You shall boil it while you say the charm Land to Water, from Water to Land, Venom come creeping here to my Hand. Cool the brew under no light save only the stars. When it is cooled, steep therein a fair white cloth which after you shall tie safely within a bag. The toad shall come into the bag and there you may take it.

Benny checked the list of things he had got ready. Bladder-wort he had not found, but he had taken a handful of weeds from the pond in the Gardens, and he thought they might do. 'A vessel'—the old saucepan with the loose handle was that, at any rate. He could not find nightshade, of course, but he had looked it up and the main thing seemed to be that it was poisonous. He had been told that the corkwood tree in the Gardens was poisonous, too, and had broken off a small spray of leaves that very afternoon while he and Rupert were coming home. His chicken claw instead of the ground-pigeon's; his slough of the adder—he was counting on that to make up for all the rest. He had a clean handker-chief as the fair white cloth; and his magic-bag seemed the very thing to tie it in safely, now that he had taken out the Australian flag and other things that were usually there. He would brew his spell tomorrow night, because then his father was going to play cards at the Youngs' place. Benny had arranged to be left at home under Mrs Chafer's ear instead of going to spend the evening with Rupert, Selina and Greg.

He put all the things away in a shoe-box in his ward-robe, got into bed and switched off the light. He reminded himself that he need not work the spell at all if he didn't happen to feel like doing it. Tomorrow night he would very likely decide not to, after all. Probably he would put the whole shoe-box into the garbage-can, just as it was. 'Venom come creeping . . .' Even if he did try it, of course, the spell would not work. He did not even have the right things, except the adder's slough . . . '. . . here to my Hand.' Toads were really even tamer than frogs. Most toads hardly jumped at all . . .

Outside in the shadows, Selina's cat went by. It was looking for a safer home for its family, away from the teasing of Net-Nets and the prying of children. It paused for a moment under Benny's window, twitching its tail. But a cat knows a real magician from an amateur. The cat went prowling on until it came to the lighted window where Ernest Hawke was at work on the afternoon's film. Soon, by some mysterious route, it had reached the porch-roof. It sat under the wing of the great white eagle and fixed its golden eyes on the window above.

In Arrow Place, Sir Mortimer's car was still parked outside the hoardings. It had been there for a long time now. No policeman had noticed it inside the narrow lane, though the workmen had when they straggled by on their way home. They had exchanged knowing nods and quiet jokes, for the car was so shiny and important that they all hoped it had broken down. No one knew where Sir Mortimer was. Mrs Ash was a little offended that he had not rung to say he would be late after all, but Sir Mortimer Wyvern was a busy and important man. If something unexpected arose, he had a right to stay out to dinner without consulting his staff.

The car simply stayed there, a dull gleam in the darkness.

Chapter 9

The city trod heavily down on the land, crushing it under its concrete feet. Yet under the city, strong and silent, lay the living rock; and in caverns and crevices within the rock lived the Nyols, old things of the land. They were small and stone-grey and shadowy. They crowded around

Sir Mortimer Wyvern and looked at him with bright, childish eyes, chuckling happily.

'I tell you,' Sir Mortimer said peevishly and for the fiftieth time, 'I will not wrestle with you!' He had not shouted since he had made his first ten thousand dollars, but now his voice was growing shrill and high. It echoed back from the rock. His neat, expensive suit and his smooth, expensive hands were rusty with rock-dust. 'You must release me at once!' shrilled Sir Mortimer. 'I have to prepare for a very important meeting.'

Meeting, echoed the rocks; *very-meeting-very-important-meeting-very . . .*

The little Nyols chuckled like the soft rumbling of stones. They were simple creatures, not very clever, but bright with the happy mischief of children. 'You wrestle,' they insisted.

Sir Mortimer shrugged pettishly.

One of the Nyols brought a flat stone on which there lay, curled up, a dozen fat grubs of a sort that no one knew except the Nyols. The Nyol offered them to Sir Mortimer.

'You eat,' they all said kindly in their soft, rumbling voices.

Sir Mortimer was very hungry indeed. Ten hours ago he had looked at those grubs with anger and hatred; now he looked with a hungry sort of despair. He looked back at the crowd of stone-grey faces and bright, simple eyes all around him. 'If I eat one,' he bargained, 'will you let me go?'

The happy Nyols chuckled. 'Let you go! Yes! We let you go!' The words went through the crowd like echoes through the rocks. 'Yes—let you go—eat.'

Sir Mortimer took up one of the grubs and shut his eyes tight. He thrust the fat thing into his mouth—and opened his eyes in astonishment. The grub tasted like chicken gently fried in butter, herbs and wine. He had never eaten anything better. He took another grub, and the Nyols chuckled and chattered in deep, soft voices. Sir Mortimer ate all the grubs very quickly.

'There,' he said in a stronger voice. 'Now you must let me go.'

'Let you go. Yes,' said the Nyols. The words went through the crowd, all about the cavern. 'You wrestle with us,' they said.

Sir Mortimer grasped his head in both hands.

After school on Tuesday afternoon, when the children had changed and gone to the Gardens to play, Selina showed Rupert and Benny the kittens. First she made them promise not to tell anyone; not to come playing with the kittens when she wasn't with them; to be very careful not to hurt them, or frighten their mother. Benny promised all these things quickly and soberly. Rupert said, 'Oh all right, Selina, do you think everyone else is as nutty as you? Are you going to show us or aren't you?'

So Selina led them to the top of the big rock, where she lay down and put her hand into the slit. She was holding a crust she had kept on purpose, to bribe the mother cat; but this time the cat was not at home. Selina counted five kittens, and was able to draw out three so that each of the children could hold one. They held them gently and gazed at the little round heads pushing blindly from side to side, and the tiny ears that seemed to have got there by mistake. Selina's was the purplish-grey one again, Rupert's was black like its mother, and Benny's was a patchwork of black and white. While they held the kittens, stroking them with one finger or letting them tangle their claws in sweaters, Rupert told Benny the unbelievable story of Selina's meeting with the Minister and how she had led him out of the Gardens through the fence. It had seemed quite natural to Selina at the time, but she giggled a good deal while listening to Rupert tell about it. Rupert giggled too, and even Benny went 'Hoo-hoo-hoo'.

Dinner was a quick meal for the Potters that evening, because Mr and Mrs Potter were going out. Greg was the only one who ate absently, without noticing the sense of hurry. He seemed to be in a heavy mood; but his family knew that this was really a deep, still excitement because of the comet that was now so near.

'What time?' asked his father, to show his sympathy.

'Nine o'clock,' said Greg at once. 'Somewhere over Cremorne or Taronga.'

'We'll take a look from Youngs' window,' Mr Potter promised.

'You'll have a better view from there than here,' said Greg, and withdrew into silence.

'Greg,' said Selina, and had to say it again. 'Greg! Will you wake us up at nine o'clock when the comet comes?'

'Wake you up?' said Greg, staring at her. 'If you want to see it you'll come, I reckon.'

'I'm going to bed straight away,' Selina told Rupert while they were washing up. 'So I won't be sleepy when it comes.' This was the first cunning move in her plan to put back the Minister's paper-knife.

'You'll only just be asleep when it does come, then— it'll be here at nine. I'm just going to read in bed while I wait; then I can see when Greg goes out, and whip out after him.'

This suited Selina very well, for if Rupert was reading in bed she could easily slip out through the living-room.

'Greg!' she said scornfully. 'He'll be out on the roof all the time, as soon as Mum and Dad go.'

Mr and Mrs Potter came to say good night, looking a little strange dressed up for visiting. 'Now don't you bother Greg,' Mrs Potter warned the children. 'You just leave him alone tonight, and behave yourselves.' Selina and Rupert saw their parents off by the front door while Greg wandered restlessly out to the roof.

As soon as the washing up was finished Selina did go to bed, and closed her door. She knew she could open it again quietly when she was ready. She left her jeans and sweater on; if Rupert did come in and see, she would say it was on account of the comet coming. She had the paper-knife tucked inside her sweater sleeve, and she switched her light off to keep Rupert away. She heard him go into the other room with Greg—and follow him out to the roof—and come in with him again. She hoped they would settle down soon; she needed only a few minutes of quiet. She lay in the dark and waited, watching the coloured lights wash over her room, for what seemed a very long time.

The Nyols crowded round Sir Mortimer with happy smiles. They were pleased because he had eaten some more grubs; they had never had a guest with such a good appetite. 'You wrestle,' they urged him.

Sir Mortimer looked at them hopelessly. He had given up lecturing them about his important meeting, and explaining how the city was depending on him to keep it fed with cars. They had only listened politely and urged him again to wrestle.

'Oh—very well,' he said sulkily, and took off his coat. He laid it on the rock and at once half a dozen Nyols clustered round it, peeping and poking, crawling under it and into its sleeves. The rest of them shuffled and skipped like shadows, and filled the cavern with a rumble of chuckles. It was absurd to think of a grown man wrestling with one of these little grey shadows, though Sir Mortimer did not think of it in quite that way. He thought how absurd and annoying it was that Sir Mortimer Wyvern should be forced to wrestle at all.

One small, stone-grey creature was pushed forward to meet him. Sir Mortimer bent to grasp it. In a second he found himself flat on the rock, jarred all through by the fall. The Nyols rolled about in joy and kicked their feet. Their eyes shone like crystals.

Selina waited in her bedroom till she was sure it must be nearly time for the comet. Greg had been out on the roof for so long now, that it seemed he must be going to stay there. Rupert seemed to have given up following him about and was waiting in bed, either reading or asleep. Selina got up, and very quietly put on her sandshoes.

She crept to the living-room and peered at the face of the big clock there. Eight o'clock—only eight! It was earlier than she had meant to be, but she was not going to creep back now. She sneaked to the front door, opened it and clicked the catch to keep it open. She would be back so quickly that no one would notice. She went out of the door and down the stairs, feeling her way step by step and not making a sound. At the foot of the stairs she opened one more door and closed it behind her. Now she was on the top floor of the Department, and a little noise would not matter.

It was darker than she had thought. She stood still for a minute, getting used to it and feeling where she was. She could feel the great stone walls about her, and the stairwells plunging down through all the floors. She was in a passage here, she remembered, with rooms on both sides where the daytime people worked. That was why no light came in from the street. If you went through one of the doors on the right and looked out of a window beyond, you would be able to see Benny's bedroom window. That faint grey light a little way ahead was from one of the stairwells; the light came from the courtyard, through the big windows above the stairs. Just beyond the stairs was a lift that would take you down to the second floor and let you out very near the Minister's room. Selina felt better when she had it all fixed in her mind. She really would be just a few minutes now—only the Department was so large at night, and so very still. Like someone not breathing. The night-time humming of the city sounded far away.

She went to the grey light, and past it to the lift. She felt about on the panel and pressed the top button. High on the wall, red-lit numbers flicked on and off as the lift slid up from floor to floor—then came a green light, and the ting of a bell. There was a hushing noise as the lift doors slid open—and Selina was startled by the light that was on in the lift. She got in, dazzled, and pressed the button marked '2'. Perhaps she could not have found the right button without the light, yet it made her feel as though a lot of people were watching. She could feel the Minister's knife hard inside her sleeve.

The lift stopped, the doors slid open, and Selina darted out like a lizard. The doors of the lift closed behind her but she was still in the light. It was only rather dimmer than in the lift. Then she saw that a light had been left on in this corridor. She didn't want the light, it shouldn't be on; she would turn it off as she passed the switch.

At the end of the corridor was the Minister's room, and beside it the dark entrance to a narrower passage. That was where she and Rupert had seen old Harry fighting with the polisher. There seemed to be some more light coming from the Minister's outer room, but Selina guessed that would be coming from the street. She went quickly towards it, switching off the corridor light as she passed, and slipped into the Minister's outer room. She was breathing rather hard, so she stood still for a moment; and that was when she saw the line of light along the edge of the Minister's inner door.

At the same moment she heard the Minister's voice. 'Tom? . . . Yes, I'm in the Department office, and I'm just leaving . . . No, thanks, I'll walk. It's only a step to the Party Rooms from here, and I feel like a stroll through the Domain . . . Yes, that's what I wanted to ask you. Will you ask the copper to leave the back gate unlocked for me? . . . Thanks, Tom. I'll see you in ten minutes.'

Selina's mind and Selina's legs went into a scurry. He was there! He was talking on the telephone! He was just leaving!—She was in the dark passage round the corner. She stood flat against the wall, pressing her hands against her chest. The Minister's door opened; light fell into the corridor and disappeared as he switched it off. He came out, a dark figure making an annoyed sound as he found the corridor in darkness. That light came on again. There was the ting of a bell and the hushing of the lift doors. He was gone, and Selina was shaking.

After a minute her breathing steadied down to a normal panting, as if she had been running. After another minute her mind had steadied down too. She wanted to be back in bed instead of in this grey-dark passage; but the Minister's knife was in her sleeve and his door was just around the corner. She went back to the outer room. If the inner one were locked she would push the knife under the door and race home to bed. She tried the door, and it opened.

More yellow light came into this room from the street. Selina could see the shining surface of the Minister's desk. Suddenly she was angry with him. Last night in the Gardens he had been so nice, and now here he was going off to that meeting at the Party Rooms just as Ernest Hawke had said. And he had given her an awful fright, too. She laid his paper-knife, his ivory paper-knife, beside his silver ink-well and hoped it would puzzle him badly. Then, defiantly, she opened one of his glass doors, propped it with his waste-paper basket for safety, and marched out on his balcony. She would just stand there for a minute; and he would never know that Selina Potter had stood on his balcony in the night, looking out at the twinkling lights of the city.

There was a sound demanding to be heard. A special, important sound, somewhere in the street. It was a small sound, but so shrill that it carried clearly through the cold night air. A bus roared in the street somewhere, and then a car passed. Selina waited for another moment of quiet, and heard the sound again—a shrill pipe of fear coming out of the night.

'A kitten!' cried Selina, whirling about.

She raced inside, knocking over the waste paper basket and banging the Minister's inner door, raced down the lighted corridor, and held her finger on the lift-button till the doors hushed open. She did not hear the wrapped-up silence of the Department, or feel the waiting offices. 'Hurry up!' she said to the lift.

On the top floor she raced up the stairs, not bothering to close the door behind her and noticing only by accident that the big clock said ten past eight. It had been a long ten minutes, but Selina was only thankful that it was still early. She threw herself into the boys' bedroom, and it was only by good fortune that Greg was still on the roof.

Rupert was in bed looking drowsy. He too had kept his sweater and jeans on, ready for the comet. Selina hurled herself at the bed.

'One of the kittens is down in the street crying,' she said. 'Are you coming?' Rupert sat up with a jerk, knocking his book to the floor. 'Well, hurry up,' said Selina. 'It'll be squashed flat, like Skit.'

Rupert's feet were already on the floor. 'Selina, you clot!' he cried in alarm. 'You can't go out there now! What d'you think Greg's going to say?'

'Has he been out on the roof all the time? Since eight o'clock?'

'I suppose so,' Rupert admitted.

'Well, then. He won't come in again till the comet

comes, and we'll only be ten minutes. Are you coming or not?'

'You can't *go*, Selina.' Even while he said it, Rupert was facing facts and groping for his slippers. What else could he do? Tell Greg—and start one of those rows that nobody ever forgets. For no one could make Selina leave that kitten in the street; Greg would really have to tie her up. And on the night of the comet, too, when it was almost due and Greg would miss seeing it come. That wasn't real.

'I'm going,' said Selina. 'I'll go through the living-room and out the side door. There's another key in that little office near the door.' She had turned away.

'Selina, stop!' ordered Rupert, coming after her. He could ring the Youngs and tell his father—but that wasn't real either. It would mean exactly the same sort of row, only worse.

'No one would want you to leave a kitten to be squashed,' Selina argued.

Rupert had followed her through the living-room, barely noticing that the front door was already open. He could ring up the police and ask them to bring his sister home—that was even less real than the other things he couldn't do.

'It's not even a kitten at all, I bet,' he said angrily, following her through dark passages to a different lift. 'Anyhow, if you can hear it, what about the mother cat? What's *she* supposed to be doing?'

'Hunting for food, of course,' said Selina. 'Or she might be looking after the others. She's got five. She mightn't even miss this one.'

'It probably isn't even her kitten.'

'I don't care if it's not,' said Selina, leaving the lift and heading for the office where the key was kept. 'And anyway, it is. How many kittens *are* there in the city, for heaven's sake?'

'It's probably crawling with them,' grumbled Rupert. '—Leave the key on the *inside*, nitwit—do you want everyone to see it? And close the door. It won't lock.'

He had known it all along. This was real life, not some half-wit story. There was nothing he could do but go with her.

Chapter 10

Out in the street it was much lighter than inside the Department. Rupert felt like an escaping convict caught in a searchlight beam, and cringed. Selina did not notice the light at all. She was listening for that high, thin crying—listening till she could almost feel her ears reaching out on each side.

'You can't hear it down here like you can up . . . there,' she said. She had very nearly said 'up on the Minister's balcony', and was glad she had stopped in time. She thought Rupert could probably not stand a shock like that.

'Where was it coming from?' he asked, still crossly.

Selina hesitated. 'That way . . . I think,' she said, pointing towards the Quay.

'Come on, then.'

They walked along the side of the Department, listening as they went. By the time they reached the cross-street they had heard the crying twice, and judged that they would have to cross the street. It was so quiet that they did not bother to wait for the traffic lights. They had just begun to cross when they heard the crying again.

Selina was puzzled. 'It's higher up than us,' she said.

'You can't tell with that kind of noise, especially at night.' Rupert still felt as though his father's eyes were boring into his back, but there was also the feeling of wickedness and adventure. He found he could not keep on being cross. The old grey building loomed ahead, its white vase-things standing up against the sky. There was one lighted window from which yellow light fell across the great eagle on the porch-roof. 'Ernest Hawke,' said Rupert. 'Doing our film, I'll bet.'

Selina looked up. It was not the window that she saw, but the kitten. The light from Mr Hawke's window fell on it, clinging with its claws to the edge of the porch-roof and dangling down over the pavement.

'How did it get there?' cried Selina, and sprang up the steps. Before Rupert could even cry out she had climbed up as she had done once before and stood balanced, grasping the roof with one hand and the kitten with the other. The kitten continued to cling with all its might to the roof. Selina, having both hands busy, could do nothing but stand there.

Rupert gaped, but only for a second. The top of the ground-floor window was still open, since Selina was standing on it, and there was Mr Hawke's light above. Rupert leapt for the front door, tried it, pounded on it, then sprang back to the pavement, feeling in his pocket. He found a large nail and threw it with all his force at the window. It struck with a clank. Rupert did not care if it broke the glass.

In a moment the window opened and Ernest Hawke looked out. He did not appear startled to see Selina and a kitten dangling from the roof so late at night. He had seen this sort of thing before, and nothing could startle him a second time. 'Hang on,' he called, quite calmly. 'I'm coming down, all right?'

Rupert pranced urgently in the street. The kitten squeaked even more pitifully. The door of the building opened, Mr Hawke strode out and grasped Selina firmly round the jeans. With this support she was able to use both hands to unhook the kitten and pass it down to Rupert, who had climbed to the base of a column. Mr Hawke then hauled Selina down like a flag.

'I wish you'd tell me next time,' he said fretfully. 'I could have had a camera ready. What now, Miss Potter?'

'We'll have to take it home,' said Selina. Rupert could hardly believe his good fortune.

'Yes,' he said warmly, 'and pretty quick, too, before Greg finds we're gone. And thanks, Mr Hawke—she's so screwy you never know what she'll do next.'

Mr Hawke smiled a very little and watched Selina.

'Take it back to its home, not ours,' she explained to Rupert. 'We couldn't keep it, it's too young. We couldn't feed it.' She took the kitten from him (it was her own purplish-grey one) and turned accusingly to Mr Hawke. 'It's a wonder you didn't hear it, just under your window. I did from right up there.'

'I never hear anything when I'm working,' he explained. 'Nothing short of a window breaking, that is. Just as well, too. I'd only have done something stupid like ringing up the fire brigade.'

Rupert was hopping urgently again. 'Selina, don't be a clot,' he commanded. 'You can't put it back in the Gardens now! You'll have to keep it till morning.'

'It might be dead by morning,' Selina threatened grimly, and turned again to Mr Hawke. 'Have you got the time, please?'

'Eight-twenty,' he told her gravely.

'See?' said Selina to Rupert. 'Only ten minutes since I heard it, and we can easily put it back in another ten minutes. Unless you're going to waste a lot of time first. You know Greg will stay on the roof till the comet comes; and even if he does go in, he'll only think you've gone to the bathroom or something.'

Now it was Rupert who turned to Mr Hawke, for he knew that any right-minded adult would take over the job of sending Selina back to bed. He had not properly understood that Ernest Hawke was different, as Selina always had.

'When you say "take it home",' he was saying to Selina, 'don't you think it was probably home already?

I don't know much about kittens, but it doesn't seem to me,' and he peered at the tiny head bobbing blindly against Selina's hand, 'that this one could have got up there by itself. I'd say its mother must have put it there.'

'It was a stupid place, then,' Selina declared. 'She'll have to find another place or leave them where they were. They can easily crawl out under that wing, and then they'll just fall off the roof.'

'In that case,' said Mr Hawke, 'we'd better get a move on, all right?'

Rupert heaved a sigh that turned into a groan. Then, since there was no help for it, he began to lead the way. At least they could go through some lanes that he knew; they were dark, but they were a little shorter. He went ahead at a fast trot, and Selina and Ernest Hawke strolled after him. Selina was adjusting her opinion of Mr Hawke: he was unreliable about demonstrations, and about car-parks in the Botanical Gardens, but he seemed to be quite sound about kittens. Mr Hawke was wondering how Selina proposed to explain its duty to the mother cat.

Hurrying ahead down the dark lane, Rupert heard a familiar sound and ran. Another kitten was mewing behind a garbage-can. Rupert gathered it up and waited for Selina. Somehow he felt better about the whole venture, now that he too had found a kitten to take back. He peered at it closely. It was the black-and-white one.

'Whatever is she *doing* with them?' Selina said crossly when she saw it.

Mr Hawke shook his head. 'Careless. She'll have to be told.'

Selina peeped up at him, not sure whether he was teasing her or not. After a minute she said, 'You were right about that meeting. They're having it tonight.'

He nodded. 'There goes another slice of the Gardens.'

'Don't you care, then? You said it was magic, the stuff you do. You said you were a magician.'

He smiled and took her elbow to hurry her across Macquarie Street while the lights were green. 'You're forgetting—magicians only work magic to suit themselves. Nobody's paying me to cook Sir Mortimer Wyvern's goose.' They had reached the nearest fence of the Gardens; he waited to see how the children proposed to get in, and followed when they turned along the fence towards the Domain. The darkness of the Gardens, the only true darkness in the city, lay on their left. They could feel it there, and see black shapes of branches, and hear a whispering of fountains.

'I suppose,' said Ernest Hawke, 'magicians might work a bit of magic to please a friend sometimes. What did you have in mind? A demonstration?'

'You said it was the right time—before things are settled.' Neither of them was quite sure which was teasing the other.

'You need people for a demonstration,' he reminded her. 'Where would you get them from now? Walk along the street explaining until you'd found enough people to come with you? The meeting would be over by the time you'd collected ten people.'

'We couldn't anyway,' Selina said sadly. 'We're not supposed to know. We'd just get somebody into trouble.'

'A problem of ethics. You'll never make a magician if you're going to get tangled up in ethics.'

He held forth on this subject while they walked through the almost-dark of the Domain, and the kittens squirmed in Rupert's and Selina's hands. A light showed through the branches of the old figs on their right, from an upstairs room where a group of important men were waiting for Sir Mortimer and the Minister. A few hundred yards behind them on the roof of the Department Greg was gazing to the north and east, waiting for the comet. A little nearer than that, at his window under the plaster shield, Benny was cooling a saucepan with a torn paper bag over it to protect it from the city's lights. Somewhere in the Domain the Minister was walking towards that light in the Party Rooms. Like a knight carrying his lady's glove into battle, the Minister was remembering a little girl with a kitten, the white figure of 'Summer' hidden in the bushes, and a row of iron bars for letting people through. Deep under the ground, in a cavern in the ancient rock, Sir Mortimer Wyvern sat exhausted while the Nyols drifted about him.

He had wrestled desperately, like one of Selina's kittens wrestling with a tornado. He had wrestled with an endless number of joyful Nyols, until he was quite exhausted and they had let him stop. They had given him more grubs, smiling with pleasure while he ate them. He had put his dusty coat on again; but his trousers were torn, his hair wild, his shiny shoes scuffed and dull, his fingernails broken and his hands black with dirt.

'You must let me go,' he pleaded hoarsely. 'A very important meeting . . .'

'You go,' they agreed, for they were on the point of forgetting all about him. They were moving about restlessly and muttering in a soft rumble. Their eyes shone with an older light. They felt the coming of the comet.

In the Gardens, too, there was a restlessness of waiting.

Selina, Rupert and Ernest Hawke all felt it as soon as they had scrambled between the rusted bars. It did not feel at all as it had felt last night when Selina was with the Minister. It felt as though it had no time for them and wanted them gone. There was a brooding, urgent silence as Selina and Rupert ran to the rock and put the kittens back. The hairy little Net-Net crouched away from them, ignoring them. In the branches overhead, silent shadows were clinging and waiting. The Pot-Koorok had come out of the pond and sat on the edge, dangling its webbed feet and staring at the sky.

Selina and Rupert ran back to the fence as quickly as they could. A dog, curled up in a thicket of oleanders, watched them go and said nothing. It was the dog Selina had met last Saturday, and it often spent the night in the Gardens. The bushes were warm, and it was easy for a dog to get itself locked in. Tonight the dog's eyes were alert and its ears moved uneasily.

'That was a bit creepy,' Rupert confessed, when they had put the iron bars back into place. He and Selina set out for home at an easy trot that they knew would get them there quickly. Ernest Hawke's long strides kept up without seeming to hurry. He knew they had taken a good deal longer than the ten minutes Selina had allowed, but he only kept on talking about Public Relations, ethics and demonstrations. They did not know when they passed the cat, on its way back for another kitten. The cat was not worried by that urgency of waiting in the Gardens. It did not belong to this old waiting land. Its tail twitched only for the magic that uses other people's minds for the good of the magician.

Ernest Hawke was still holding forth about this sort of

magic as he and the children crossed Macquarie Street on their way home.

'You need people for a demonstration, all right? And it takes people a while to make up their minds. That's what a magician has to work on, remember: their minds. Now, if you could find a lot of people without minds, you could stage your demonstration outside that meeting tonight and very likely do some good. They think their secret is safe, you see, and they wouldn't be ready for you. You'd startle their guilty consciences.'

Selina gave a giggle, half teasing and half excited. They were coming safely home, their adventure over; she could see the old grey building ahead, and the bulk of the Department over the way. 'I can find you a lot of people without minds,' she told Ernest Hawke 'All the shop windows have them.'

He looked a little startled. None of them saw a faint, pale light reaching down to touch them; only Greg, high on a roof across the street, saw the comet rise. Rupert, Selina and Mr Hawke heard a shrill, familiar crying from the porch-roof of the grey building, and Selina broke into a run.

'Oh no!' she cried. 'It's another one!'

The kitten, the black one, could just be seen squirming out past the eagle's wing; it was not in any danger yet.

'Quick!' cried Selina.

'That cat,' said Ernest Hawke severely, 'has no maternal sense and no judgement . . . Move your wing, bird.'

Slowly, stiffly, the great plaster eagle moved its wing a little forward and a little lower, making a safe wall to keep the kitten in. The comet had risen, pale and cold, above the city lights. A few people watched for it; a lot of others never saw it at all.

Old Harry did not see it as he sat by a window reading his paper, but its light touched him all the same.

Harry was staring at an advertisement that showed a new and wonderful polisher. He stared at it, and his face suddenly twisted. 'If I had that old thing here,' muttered Harry fiercely, 'I'd take an axe to it.' And at that moment inside a dark cupboard in the empty Department there was a clanging noise. There was a splintering, and a muffled crash. The old polisher was in pieces, quite beyond repair.

In Hyde Park a shabby old figure with a limp briefcase was making a late round of the garbage-bins. That faint, far light touched his fingers as they flickered in and out again; the old man started, and thrust that hand into the pocket of his shabby coat. He flitted away, from shadow to shadow, going home as quickly as he could, and inside his pocket his fingers were clenched like steel on a ten-dollar note. He could hardly believe it.

The comet-light had touched Benny, too, as he sat on the storeroom step with his magic-bag beside him; and at first Benny was gripped by horror. He had cooked his strange broth in the old saucepan with the loose handle, bending over it anxiously. It had smelt like weedy chicken-broth, old and evil. He had recited the charm almost without thinking, as a means of timing the cooking, and then had covered it with its paper cap and carried it to his bedroom to cool on the window-sill. The cooling took longer than anything; but when the outside of the saucepan felt cool he had taken it, for safety, down to the darkness of the storeroom. There he had dipped his fair white handkerchief into the brew, squeezed it out gently, and put it into his magic-bag, knotting the drawstring round the top. Then he had poured the brew away quickly down a grating in the courtyard, wrapped the bones and mush in paper and put the parcel in the garbage-can, and sat down on the storeroom step to wait. He had no idea how long it would take, but he preferred to wait on the storeroom step at least until his father came home.

He did not see the comet rise. The courtyard walls round about, and the smoky-rose glow of the city lights above, shut out the sight. But its pale, cold light filtered in though he did not see it. The first thing he noticed was a fragrance, sweet and sharp, and he looked about in a puzzled way. He saw the thin shape of his father's sooty gardenia and then he saw, here and there in its darkness, something dimly white. He got up from the step to look. The gardenia was suddenly in flower.

Benny stood over it, frowning and puzzled, until he heard a peculiar sound from the step where he had been sitting. He could tell what the sound was, though his mind tried not to know; he stood with his back to it until he could not bear to have it behind him any longer. It was the sound of his magic-bag flopping around on the step: flopping and flapping because something was struggling to get out.

Benny walked back in a stiff-legged way and stood over it. It was quite a big bag really, but it was filled tight with whatever was struggling about inside. Benny would never have believed any toad could be as big as that, or that it would struggle so much, He was horrified at its struggling, but he could not untie the bag; he could not touch it. He just stood there and watched until the knotted string slipped off the mouth of the bag and it burst open. Something began to struggle out.

At first he thought it really was the most enormous toad or frog, because it had that sort of skin. It gleamed a little, and seemed to be a muddy green colour. Then, as the thing came out of the bag—more and more of it, so that it could never really have fitted in at all—he saw it was more like some sort of person. It stood upright, about as high as his waist. It had a pear-shaped head and body with very little neck, thin legs rather bent at the knee, and webbed feet. The arms hung down loosely, with rather large hands for its size. The fingers were flattened, but they looked useful and clever. Its frog-like face looked indignant and insulted. Benny could not know that the thing was a Pot-Koorok. He could only think that he would never try another spell, not in a thousand years.

Pot-Kooroks are practical jokers, and all practical jokers hate to have jokes played on them. This Pot-Koorok lived in a little stream that had once flowed through a forest, but which long ago the city had gripped in a concrete fist and turned into an underground drain. Like the other old creatures of the land, the Pot-Koorok had felt the passing of a thousand years and the coming of a magic hour. It had been making its slow way to the landward end of its prison (for it was a freshwater spirit, and could not simply slip through a grating into the sea) when suddenly the hour began, and it found itself struggling inside a black bag. Cross and upset, it hurried out of the courtyard, half running and half hopping on its skinny bent legs and leaving wet footprints like a very large frog's. Somehow it went over the closed gate; but before it did so it turned its head and looked at Benny.

And suddenly he saw how comically huffy and offended it looked. His heart lightened in one bound, and he began to run after it.

The Pot-Koorok was looking for an open space, and something more real than asphalt or concrete under its feet; but most of all it was looking for a break in the electric dazzle of city lights, and a sight of the sky. It took the first way at hand, down the street towards the Department, and then on past. Benny had to run hard to keep it in sight. He had not even yet seen the comet, for the city tried to keep it out with a glare of little lights. Yet that thin, thousand-year light had touched the Pot-Koorok. It saw darkness, and trees on a skyline, and leapt uphill to the Botanical Gardens.

Benny did not see it go. Instead, he saw Rupert and Selina standing in the street with Ernest Hawke.

Chapter 11

If you have just worked a spell that produced a Pot-Koorok, or if you have just seen a plaster eagle obey the command of a magician, you are not as surprised as you normally would be to meet your friends at an unusual time. It takes more than that to surprise you.

Benny simply crossed the street and said, 'Hi.' Rupert said, 'Benny! What's up with you now?' Then they both fixed their eyes on Ernest Hawke.

He hardly seemed surprised at all by the eagle's obedience. He was looking at it in a pleased and satisfied way, as if he had proved something that he had always suspected. He looked taller and thinner than usual, his beard longer and blacker, and his eyes had a glitter you could see in the dark. None of them knew that Hawke the magician had been touched by comet-light; on the other hand, the children had all been touched by it too. They did not run screaming for home as they might otherwise have done. They felt the imminence of magic and were awed, but they accepted it.

'Show me your people without minds,' Hawke was saying grandly to Selina, 'and I will give you your demonstration. Just wait till I get my keys.'

He already had a key, for he unlocked the door of the building with it and went inside. Selina waited dumbly. Rupert and Benny, now that that towering figure was away, began to gabble reports to each other.

'—and he made it move its wing. Look it's different.'

'It's not just him, there's something else too. There was this spell in this book I bought . . .'

'I knew there was something when we were in the Gardens. Creepy . . . !'

'—like a frog-person. I chased it right down here. It was nice, though.'

Ernest Hawke came back. He was dangling a huge bundle of keys tied with a leather thong. 'My collection,' he told them proudly. 'Used to be a hobby of mine—keys from everywhere. I'll be surprised if there's not a key to any door in the city. Now then, young lady.'

You could not argue with him when his eyes glittered like that; yet Selina did not see how anyone, even Hawke the magician, could arrange a demonstration by the beautiful, petrified people in the shop windows. There was not even a truck to carry them to the Party Rooms. She turned silently and led the way down the street. Ernest Hawke strode beside her very confidently, with the night wind stirring his beard. Benny and Rupert trailed behind, still whispering reports to each other. In the ground far under their feet the Nyols were rushing towards the Gardens, carrying Sir Mortimer Wyvern along with them willy-nilly. Farther off in the Party Rooms, where that upstairs light still shone over the Domain, a group of very important men fidgeted restlessly while they waited for Sir Mortimer who was now half an hour late. The fact that they had waited at all showed the super-importance of Sir Mortimer.

There had been a lot of telephoning that failed to find any trace of him. The lesser men of Commerce had explained all the things that might have delayed him, ranging from a change of government in a nearby country to the breakdown of his shiny, important car; but nobody thought of Nyols. Now, when the chairman looked at the clock and tapped on the table with his pencil, they could think of no more excuses at all.

'Gentlemen,' said the chairman, 'I am sure that only the most urgent and unforseen affair could have kept Sir Mortimer Wyvern from this meeting; but since it has done so, we are wasting valuable time. We will begin the meeting, and hope that Sir Mortimer may yet arrive to give us his assistance.'

The lesser men exchanged uneasy looks. They prepared themselves to do their best for Sir Mortimer's plan while still leaving it open for him to carry on if he did arrive. The Minister rubbed his hands in secret glee and gave a tiny wink at his memory of the child with the kitten.

The child herself had led Ernest Hawke to the first of the windows, where the lady in the frilly apron still stood with her hand stretched out to the stove. Selina had decided it was safest to start with a single model, like trying out the bathwater with your elbow.

Ernest Hawke squinted thoughtfully at the lady in the apron. She did not seem to excite him. 'Well,' he said, 'we need all we can get.' And he went to the closed door of the shop and fumbled with his keys.

Selina could hardly believe it when he opened the door; yet she did believe it in a second or two. Benny looked interested and thoughtful, as he did when examining a new magic trick. Rupert simply gaped. Mr Hawke went into the shop, and in a minute a door at the rear of the shop window opened. The lady at the stove turned stiffly, and walked out by herself in a petrified way. Almost at once she came walking through the door of the shop itself and stood on the pavement. The moment she stopped walking she fell into the same position as she had held in the window, with one hand stretched out as though it still rested on the stove. Mr Hawke came after her and locked the door of the shop.

The children had edged quickly away from the lady in the apron, but they kept on staring at her. She was still an ordinary shop window model in spite of having walked. Yet when real people walked past her on the pavement, they glanced at her as if she were another person and took no more notice. They took no particular notice of Ernest Hawke, either. This was all the more strange because he was now carrying a large sign that he must have found in the shop. It said SAVE! in very large red letters.

'I forgot about banners,' he explained when he saw Selina looking at it. 'Where next? We'll need to move quickly, all right?'

Selina said nothing, but her chin was up a little and and her eyes had a glint of their own. She led him a little farther down George Street, while the two boys followed and the lady in the frilly apron walked stiffly behind the boys. They stopped outside the window where the gay young women with sparkling hair were being very active in their wonderful clothes. Selina looked at Mr Hawke as if to say, I dare you. Mr Hawke clattered his keys and said 'Ah.' The lady in the frilly apron took up her pose again. To Selina it began to look stupid.

They waited while Mr Hawke went into the shop. Soon all the gay young women filed out and took up their poses on the pavement: on tiptoe, kneeling, reaching up, flinging out their arms, or bending down to pat imaginary dogs. They took up a lot of room, but the passers-by seemed to find them an ordinary crowd and moved politely aside. Selina had a good look at their stiff, two-inch eyelashes while they all waited for Ernest Hawke.

He came out with a second advertising sign. It said ASK ABOUT OUR TERMS; but he had folded back the two ends of the sign until only the word OUR could be seen. Then he looked over the crowd of young women in their poses, nodded approvingly and said, 'Next?'

Selina did not even blink, but took him straight too the window full of sun-tanned young men in polo-sweaters. 'Good, good,' he said, nodding seriously. 'We need some balance.' This time, when he brought out the young men, he had another large sign that simply said GARDENS.

'Something about gardens in winter,' he explained. 'All spread out on separate signs. Very useful. "SAVE OUR GARDENS". I think that should do.'

Selina did not answer. She was worried about the young man who had been standing with one foot on a cardboard log. He looked very unsafe out here, standing on one leg with the other in the air. She was a little anxious about the tiptoe girl, too. On the other hand the young man with the riding-whip (he had brought it with him) looked quite forceful, almost dangerous.

Ernest Hawke was saying, 'We have just about enough of your people without minds, Miss Potter. Are there any more quite near?'

'A couple, I think,' said Selina, trying to sound as casual and off-hand as he did. She took him to the window where the graceful ladies stood in their long evening gowns with their smiling escorts.

'Colourful,' he said. 'It will be a very representative demonstration. Forceful.'

Selina looked nervously at the young man with the riding-whip. She hoped it would be a peaceful demon-stration.

They collected these four and then went back by the way they had come. They went as quickly as they could, and the make-believe people went quickly too, in their petrified way. They made quite a large crowd, forcing real people off the pavement. Whenever they had to pause for a traffic light all the make-believe people fell at once into their poses; and still nobody seemed to notice anything odd.

'Some of them come from Sir Mortimer Wyvern's own shop,' Rupert pointed out. 'Won't he notice?'

'I'm afraid not,' said Ernest Hawke regretfully. His eyes were glittering brilliantly, and he seemed very confident and happy.

He insisted that Rupert, Selina and Benny must now go home. 'It's nine-twenty-five,' he told them. 'You've been out for over an hour. I'll stage your demonstration for you, but I'd rather not be arrested for kidnapping.' They cried out in protest, Rupert loudest of all, but he drew himself up tall and looked at them sternly with his eyes glittering and his beard floating in the wind, so they stopped.

'Can't we even see if the kitten's all right?' Selina asked in her injured voice.

'Very quickly, then,' he agreed; and when they reached the porch of the grey building he hoisted Selina up. There were now three kittens in the nest behind the eagle's wing. Selina also had a good look at the crowd of make-believe people in all their poses. They looked better from above: quite lively and active, not petrified at all.

By the time Mr Hawke had lifted her down, Rupert had thought of another excuse to stay a little longer.

'That traffic light in Macquarie Street's been green ever since we left Pitt Street. I've been watching. It'll turn red as soon as you get there, and it always takes a long time to change again. We'd better come that far in case you need any help. I mean, some real people might want to be in the demonstration or something.'

'That's a feeble excuse,' said Ernest Hawke, crushing him. '. . . You can come as far as the other side of Macquarie Street if you promise, on your honour, to run home as fast as you can after that. Demonstrations are no place for you. These things can get out of hand. All right?'

They promised eagerly and set off again with their procession. There did seem to be a minor traffic jam in Macquarie Street. On each side of the lights a long line of cars were held up. Horns hooted crossly, and drivers put their heads out of windows while the lights went on telling pedestrians to cross. Ernest Hawke smiled knowingly; he was sure the lights were fixed at green for his procession. In fact there was quite another reason. Skit, the lizard, his small black shape touched by comet-light, was migrating to the Botanical Gardens. It was three minutes since he had started to cross the street, and the WALK sign stayed for him, and the line of cars grew longer, until he was safe on the other side. Ernest Hawke and the children overtook him on his way and never knew it.

Then, since they had promised, the children had to stand on the pavement and watch the procession disappear without them: Hawke the magician striding in front and a long line of petrified people streaming stiffly after him; along the fence of the Gardens towards the library; over the crossings and away into the dimness of the Domain.

'I wonder if it'll work?' said Rupert.

Suddenly they all shivered. Standing alone on the

pavement while the gay, shabby city-magic of Hawke and his models disappeared, suddenly they felt something else reaching out from the dark Gardens. Something as old as the thousand-year comet and infinitely lonely. They thought they heard a crying; and for a moment they huddled together, shivering.

'I'm going home,' said Benny. 'See you.' He darted back on to the crossing, where the light was still green for pedestrians.

'Come on, Selina, quick,' said Rupert, and they both ran back too. By the time Skit had climbed the wall of the gutter, and the lights changed and the line of cars stopped hooting, they were tumbling through the side door of the Department, locking the door behind them with unsteady hands.

Though he did not reach the important meeting in the Party Rooms, Sir Mortimer Wyvern was closer than anyone knew. He reached the Botanical Gardens, borne along by a crowd of Nyols in a fever of impatience. They carried him with them by the pressure of their little grey bodies, yet they did not seem to hear his pleas to be set free or even to know that he was there. In fact they had forgotten him; for Nyols are simple creatures and can think of only one thing at a time. They had never understood about the meeting, and just now they were thinking of the comet.

They remembered how it had come before, a thousand years ago: how it had hung clear and still, the silver plume of its tail laid across the sky over the low hills dark with forest. That had been a wonder and a magic. They had seen its light on the water like a breath of silver; for nights were dark in that time, and such things could be seen. How the tribes had gazed at it, gathered on the hills and on the rocks of the shore. The small things out of rocks and streams and bush had gazed and wondered too. They had called to it and crooned to it—the Nyols who lived in the deep rocks, and the Net-Nets who lived in the rocks above the ground; the Bitarr who played secretly with dark native children, and the Tutugals who punished them when they were bad; the Pot-Kooroks, the imps of the streams, and the Turongs who tricked hunters in the bush; even the ghostly Mahrachs whose one trick was to scare people; they all had wondered at the silent, silver comet trailing its plume of light. For hundreds of years afterwards the little spirits had crept about the campfires at night, to hear the changing stories the tribes told about it. And now it was coming again, the thousand-year magic. The Nyols trembled in their eagerness, rushing by underground paths to see it.

They came out of the ground into the Botanical Gardens, bringing Sir Mortimer with them. There was air about him at last, and the wideness of night—the shapes of trees and shrubs, and the dark smoothness of lawns. He heard again the soft lapping of water on rock. Sir Mortimer stood up straight in his torn and dusty clothes, though his dusty hair hung in strands.

'Excuse me,' he said, taking deep breaths of air. 'A very important meeting . . .' They took no notice of him, and he knew that this was wrong; for he was Sir Mortimer Wyvern and they were just a crowd of grey shadows. So he spoke again, rather more pompously. 'Nine-fifteen, I see. I may just be in time.'

But the Nyols still pressed about him. They did not

mean to hold him—their game with him was over, and they did not think of him at all. They only crowded to the brink of the rock from which Selina's cat had just emerged with the last kitten.

And all that shore was crowded. The Net-Nets moved further down the rock to make room, their clawed hands folded and their sharp little faces raised to the sky. Pot-Kooroks were clustered on the stone steps, making them damp. Behind, on the lawns, stood the Bitarr with their white beards blowing in the wind. They were sturdier and more at home than the others, for there are always children to play with, white or brown. The frailest and most lost of all the creatures were those among the branches of the trees and shrubs: the Turongs, from whom the forests had gone. Here and there the shapeless Mahrach drifted. All of them, of every kind, lifted their faces to the comet.

And there it was, the ancient star, laying its plume of light along the sky. The same hills lay under it, spread with a net of lights to shut it out. You could not see its faint shine on the water because of the wrinkled yellow light of the ferries. The bush and the tribes were gone; but the ancient creatures of the land were here to watch and croon.

Sir Mortimer looked at them with disgust but spoke politely as a great man should.

'Excuse me . . .' he was saying; when the Turongs lifted their heads and began to howl. They howled with the lost, long howling of dingoes. There was a shudder and a shiver through the Gardens, and the Mahrachs sighed.

'Our star,' crooned the Nyols in soft, rumbling voices.

'That one, our star . . .' The Bitarr were crying 'Gone, gone, gone . . .' The Pot-Kooroks croaked: 'Poor feller me; poor feller me.' The Gardens were full of their mourning, and the pale light of the comet touched them gently; for they would not cry again for a thousand years and soon they would forget. In an hour, perhaps, they would chuckle and play again.

Caught in the midst of that long, sad crying, Sir Mortimer struggled hard to escape. He pushed aside small grey shadows and forced his way back from the rock, still saying 'Excuse me' from time to time out of habit. They let him go and did not resist, being busy with their crying though they were not sure why. He came out through the throng to the lawns beyond and dived quickly into a thicket of oleanders. He needed a moment to recover, and to think where the nearest telephone was.

Something moved by his foot. Not more of them!— He bent down to peer, and stretched a hand to touch. There was a large dog curled up among the oleanders; if he had trodden on it no doubt it would have bitten him, he thought sourly. He could see the whites of its eyes as it listened to the old things crying.

'Excuse me,' he said again from force of habit.

'Why should anyone excuse you, man?' said the dog.

Sir Mortimer stayed as he was, bending down towards it with his hand stretched out. His torn clothes hardened, and the strands of hair on his forehead; his feet were rooted in the earth. His eyes were fixed forever in a look of startled disbelief.

Sir Mortimer Wyvern had turned into stone.

Chapter 12

Rupert and Selina tumbled in through the side door of the Department as if someone were chasing them. Rupert's hands were almost shaking as he locked the door and put the key away. Then both stood still for a moment while the echo of that lonely crying in the Gardens died away, along with the sound of Benny's feet racing home through the night. Slowly, the quiet strength of the old Department grew up around them, massive and safe. They felt the half-dark hall spreading away to the black-dark empty offices. They remembered where the lift was. They were home.

It was like waking up from a dream that was too real, or escaping from a game that had grown too exciting. Things came back into their minds—ordinary things that had dropped out of sight under the glittering eye of Hawke the magician. They remembered Greg and hoped very much that he was still standing on the roof, watching the comet. They crept quietly into the lift, quietly up the stairs, and very quietly through the front door. In the living-room they stood helpless for a moment, unable to believe that everything could be so normal. Then Selina crept to the back door and returned.

'He's still there,' she whispered. 'He wouldn't be just standing there if he knew we'd gone out, would he?'

'Of course he wouldn't,' said Rupert. He was peering at the big clock. 'Twenty to ten,' he whispered. 'That's . . . that's *exactly* an hour and a half!'

'An hour and a half!'

They looked at each other; and suddenly, silently, they began to giggle. They kept on for nearly a minute, and somehow the giggling put everything right. When it began, they hardly knew what to believe; they were poised between comet-magic and ordinary life. When the giggling was over, they had come down on the side of ordinary life. They would never forget this fantastic evening, but neither would they believe in it. Their minds had decided to turn it into a secret, pretended joke.

From now on, whenever something reminded them of it, Selina would giggle and Rupert would say 'Selina, you clot!'

There were only one or two doubting moments left. For instance, as they went out of the living-room Selina switched the light on; that was for Benny, alone and perhaps still shaken, so that he would have a friendly light to look at. They left it on and ran out to the roof, crying with wicked innocence, 'Where is it, Greg? Show us the comet!'

Greg had not noticed the time, of course. He simply thought he had had ten minutes or so alone with the comet, and was glad of it. When the children did arrive he was very patient, and helped them up to a safe place on the wall by the skylights and showed them the comet.

There it was, low in the sky; not like a sky-rocket at all, but like a great star burning with still, white fire. You could not see it moving, yet you seemed to see a tremendous force in the misty, fiery trail it had left on the sky. You could see, too, why the city rejected it—for it had nothing to do with the city, though a little of its magic had seeped through by accident. For a time it charmed Rupert and Selina into silence.

'A thousand years,' whispered Rupert, awed. 'Gee, Greg . . .'

Greg told them some things about it that he thought they ought to know, and they listened without taking anything in. Nothing about the comet mattered except the comet itself. Yet after a while they grew restless and gave up looking at it.

'Those ones in the zoo don't like it,' Selina said uneasily, because there seemed to be a wild crying and howling that she could very nearly hear. It was better when she looked down instead of up—except that she did not like to look at the dark patch of the Botanical Gardens, either. So she and Rupert looked at the street, which they did not often see from this height. They could see quite a lot of Macquarie Street, and could follow their own pavement almost up to the corner.

They were tired and limp, yet their minds were not yet quiet enough for bed. They were still glad to have Greg near, and sat there quietly in case he should send them off. They sat there until they saw an odd-looking crowd coming down their pavement from Macquarie Street.

It was a gay, colourful crowd, but moving in a stiff and dream-like way. When it passed under a street-light there was a sparkle of fair hair and evening gowns. There was a young man who pointed with a riding-whip; and in front strode a tall, bearded figure who carried some advertising signs. Selina nudged Rupert and pointed and giggled. Rupert looked and grinned.

'Selina, you clot,' he said.

'I wonder if it worked?' Selina whispered. By the jaunty way Ernest Hawke was walking she thought it had.

'Will he get them all back in the right shops?' Rupert whispered back. Selina looked stricken for a moment; then they both laughed silently until they shook and Greg sent them to bed.

Ernest Hawke believed that the demonstration had worked very well. He also believed he had been right all along about Public Relations and advertising men, the only true magicians left in the modern world. Every magician has his own special line of magic, but tonight

Ernest Hawke had stumbled into a different line.

'It's just a knack,' he told himself. 'Might be quite useful if I can keep it up.'

He had led his demonstrators through a gate that was already unlocked, right into the grounds behind Parliament House. He had ranged them outside the Party Rooms, where they had all taken up their shop window poses, and had placed his banners in such hands as were conveniently placed to hold them. After that he only had to attract the notice of the important men at the meeting in the room above. He had done it by banging on the lid of their garbage-can and shouting angrily in as many different voices as he could.

'It was a good show,' he told Selina later. 'The copper on duty wanted to turn us out, but the big-wigs were all too nervous and they wouldn't let him. They thought an angry city had discovered their guilty plans and there might be a riot. We weren't quite the usual crowd, you see. More intelligent and lively. Impressive.'

Selina was surprised at this view of the petrified people; perhaps their shop window poses had made them look intelligent and lively. She was glad to find, when she asked, that the tiptoe girl and the young man on one leg had remained steady throughout the demonstration.

'It came at just the right moment,' Mr Hawke went on smugly. 'Stopped them cold. There'll be no more of that little scheme, you'll see. Have a Crackle-Crunch. There's all this pile left over.'

He was partly right about the demonstration; it had indeed been quite a help to the Minister. The Minister was taken by surprise, like everyone else at the meeting; but he was keyed up to battle, and his mind had worked a few seconds faster than anyone else's. For the first second he was astonished that Sir Mortimer's secret plan had been betrayed, and he wondered how. In the next second he had seen that the men of Commerce would soon blame him for the betrayal. In the third second he had got in before them.

'It was very unwise of you gentlemen,' he said severely, 'to inform the public about this meeting before a decision had been reached. I think the Government might have expected to be treated with more respect than that. And you see the result, the very natural result: the people are angry. At the first hint of a threat to the Botanical Gardens they invade the grounds of the House itself . . . That seems to be a very active demonstration, Mr Chairman, if I may say so. I suggest it should be handled with great care.'

The lesser men of Commerce looked at each other unhappily. Each one knew that he had not given away Sir Mortimer's secret, but each wondered whether George or Edward or Bill might have let a word fall in the wrong place. This uncertainty was added to the uncertainty about Sir Mortimer himself—why he had not appeared, and whether they were putting his plan forward in the way he would wish. The Minister had made good use of that uncertainty, too.

'I can't help feeling,' he would say, 'that if the position were as grave as these gentlemen suggest, Sir Mortimer Wyvern would have found some way to attend this meeting. Or at least to let us know what had happened.' Or, when an argument rose: 'Well Sir Mortimer Wyvern may yet arrive and explain this point to us.'

Every time he said it a ripple of worry would pass

through the men of Commerce; and that was a help, too. But his greatest help was to know that only he, of all these men, had climbed out of the Gardens through the rusted bars of the fence, along with a disappearing child. It gave him a sense of coolness and spirit; and the Minister fought a battle that night that was long remembered in a small, important circle.

He had his reward next morning, when he called at his office in the Department. It was an early call, for the Minister was on his way to his office in another place. He found his inner door locked, as was normal. (The catch was faulty, and had slipped off when Selina rushed out banging the door, so that it had locked behind her. The Minister simply thought he had locked the door on leaving as he had meant to do.) He opened the door with his key in the ordinary way, and went in.

The glass door to his balcony stood open. He stood in the doorway, staring at it; for it was always kept bolted on the inside because of his air-conditioning. He hurried towards it and saw, as he passed the desk, the waste-paper basket lying on its side. That drew his eyes towards the desk itself—and there, beside his silver inkwell, lay the ivory paper-knife.

The Minister picked it up. Then he looked thoughtfully about the room, and the balcony outside. He was not looking for signs of a burglar. He just thought there might be a kitten, or some trace of a hairy little person with claws.

By that time a great many people had decided that Sir Mortimer Wyvern could not simply be busy in some unexpected place; and then a great hue and cry began. The police were called in to search for him—Brown and

Ash and Mrs Ash were asked a great many questions—newspaper headlines shouted until they were hoarse. Commerce was nervous and fidgety, prices fell; but the great man's affairs were in such splendid order that the prices soon climbed back to normal. There were companies to manage Sir Mortimer's business affairs while he was away, and lawyers and agents to manage his personal affairs. These people tried to find him for a long time, but the ordinary people forgot him very soon.

The comet appeared in the sky every night for a week, and Greg saw it every night; but there were no more nights of magic. Perhaps in that first hour of comet-light there were other magical happenings in the city; if so. the city kept them hidden and no one ever heard of them, Old Harry had a new polisher and missed the old one badly. The shabby old man grew more and more intent in his search of the garbage-bins, and began to snarl a little like an angry rat; but though he spent the rest of his life in searching, he never found another ten-dollar note.

Mr Golightly was astonished to find his sooty gardenia in flower. He never forgot it, though it faded the next day. He used to talk about it to his friends in the roof-top village until they came to think of him as a man who knew a lot about gardenias. 'They're worth trying,' he used to say wisely. 'You *can* get them to flower sometimes, but you must clean every bit of the leaves.'

Benny hid his book of spells behind all the others on his shelf and never took it down again. He did not really think it had much to do with the events of that fantastic night, yet somehow he got an excited little shiver when he caught a glimpse of the book and he could not quite decide to throw it away. He could never really have worked a spell with it, anyway. For one thing, there was Ernest Hawke's demonstration, and the book had had nothing to with that. For another, Benny agreed with Rupert and Selina that the whole evening had been only a secret, pretended joke.

Ernest Hawke, on the other hand, was always sure he had greater powers than he knew or understood. Sometimes he would try, secretly, to prove them again, but he was never upset when he failed. He had worked it out that his own way of working magic through other people's minds was the way he knew and understood; the other had been just the accidental striking of a new, strange note.

'I may never strike it again in a thousand years,' he would say to Selina's cat. 'That's neither here nor there—only a magician could have struck it at all.'

The cat would arch its back and purr, for it agreed. A black cat knows by the prickling of its fur when it meets a magician. A Net-Net here or there is nothing but natural mischief and a danger to kittens, but the cat felt at home under Ernest Hawke's window. Her kittens grew up behind the wing of the plaster eagle, and when they were old enough she taught them her own mysterious routes about the city.

The Crackle-Crunch film was a great success, and all the children loved to see themselves on their own television sets, even Selina. It really seemed almost as much like magic as Hawke's demonstration, for the camera made the places look mysterious and strange instead of familiar. And the Crackle-Crunch bars seemed to have been there all the time, instead of being carried up by the climbers. And though the climbers were really Rupert, Selina and Benny, yet they looked different when that amused and confident voice said, 'They'll go anywhere for Crackle-Crunch!'

There was no more talk of a car-park in the Gardens, at least not for this time. The children went on playing there every afternoon, rushing up to the top fence whenever they heard a demonstration coming down Macquarie Street. They were watching one afternoon when Selina gave Rupert a nudge. 'When they stop walking,' she said, 'the girl in the purple sweater will kneel down, and the man in the brown coat will stand on one leg.' They, and Benny too, went off into shrieks of laughter.

They often played by the pond—and Benny would have been startled to know that two Pot-Kooroks lived there now, playing tricks on each other and taking it in turns to bubble with joy or go into an indignant huff. One day Selina, hiding from the boys behind a clump of oleanders, thought she saw a shape among them and peered through the branches.

'Rupert!' she called in a startled voice. 'Come and see!'

Rupert and Benny both came, and they all looked at the statue among the oleanders.

'Isn't it funny?' said Selina. 'I've never seen it before. It must be another one they don't like, like "Summer". Doesn't it look real?'

'I don't blame them if they don't like it,' said Rupert, frowning at the statue.

Benny said, 'I wonder what it's meant to be?'

'It looks a bit like that Sir Mortimer,' said Selina, and Rupert broke into scornful laughter.

'Selina, you clot! Sir Mortimer . . . ! With those old

torn clothes and shoes—and that look on its face! *Sir Mortimer!*'

'All right,' said Selina crossly. 'I know it's not like him really. It's just—I don't like it, anyway.'

Neither did the gardeners when they came upon the statue months later; and they too were startled to find it there at all. The oleanders were old, and their leafy depths not often disturbed. The gardeners had a hazy idea that the statue must have been put there and forgotten very long ago.

But the old things that came to the Gardens at night loved the statue. The Turongs, hiding in bushes and trees, discovered it first; the Net-Nets, Nyols and Bitarr loved it best. They grasped the hand that stretched down, climbed over the bent knee, slid down the sloping back, or sat on the shoulders and crooned. The Net-Nets combed the untidy strands of hair with their claws. Sir Mortimer had never been so loved.

For stone is stone; and men whose drills break into the living stone should take care. They may find what they do not expect.

ABOUT THE AUTHOR

Patricia Wrightson is acknowledged as one of Australia's most distinguished writers for children. Since 1956 when her first novel, *The Crooked Snake*, was published, her books have won many prestigious awards all over the world. She was awarded an OBE in 1977, the Dromkeen Medal in 1984 and the Hans Christian Andersen Medal in 1986, all for her services to children's literature. Many of her books have also been shortlisted for the Australian Children's Book of the Year Award and she has now won this award four times: in 1956 for *The Crooked Snake*, in 1974 for *The Nargun and the Stars*, in 1978 for *The Ice is Coming* and in 1984 for *A Little Fear*.

Patricia lives and writes in a beautiful stretch of the Australian bush beside the Clarence River in northern New South Wales.